Fearful

ALSO BY LAUREN ROBERTS

Powerless
Powerful: A Powerless Story
Reckless
Fearless

fearful

LAUREN ROBERTS

SIMON & SCHUSTER

London   New York   Amsterdam/Antwerp
Sydney/Melbourne   Toronto   New Delhi

First published in Great Britain in 2025 by Simon & Schuster UK Ltd

Text copyright © 2025 Lauren Roberts
POWERLESS is a trademark of Lauren's Library LLC
Map copyright © 2025 Patrick Knowles
Cover image copyright © 2025 Bob Lea
Map designed by Patrick Knowles
Cover designed by Loren Catana

This book is copyright under the Berne Convention.
No reproduction without permission.
All rights reserved.

The right of Lauren Roberts to be identified as the author of this work has been asserted by her in accordance with sections 77 and 78 of the Copyright, Designs and Patents Act, 1988.

1 3 5 7 9 10 8 6 4 2

Simon & Schuster UK Ltd
1st Floor, 222 Gray's Inn Road
London
WC1X 8HB

www.simonandschuster.co.uk
www.simonandschuster.com.au
www.simonandschuster.co.in

Simon & Schuster Australia, Sydney
Simon & Schuster India, New Delhi

A CIP catalogue record for this book is available from the British Library.

The authorised representative in the EEA is Simon & Schuster Netherlands BV, Herculesplein 96, 3584 AA Utrecht, Netherlands. info@simonandschuster.nl

HB ISBN 978-1-3985-3576-3
eBook ISBN 978-1-3985-3577-0
eAudio ISBN 978-1-3985-3578-7

This book is a work of fiction. Names, characters, places and incidents are either the product of the author's imagination or are used fictitiously. Any resemblance to actual people living or dead, events or locales is entirely coincidental.

Typeset in the UK by Sorrel Packham

Printed and Bound in the UK using 100% Renewable Electricity at CPI Group (UK) Ltd, Croydon, CR0 4YY

*To those fearful of falling — in love or otherwise —
you're braver than you know.*

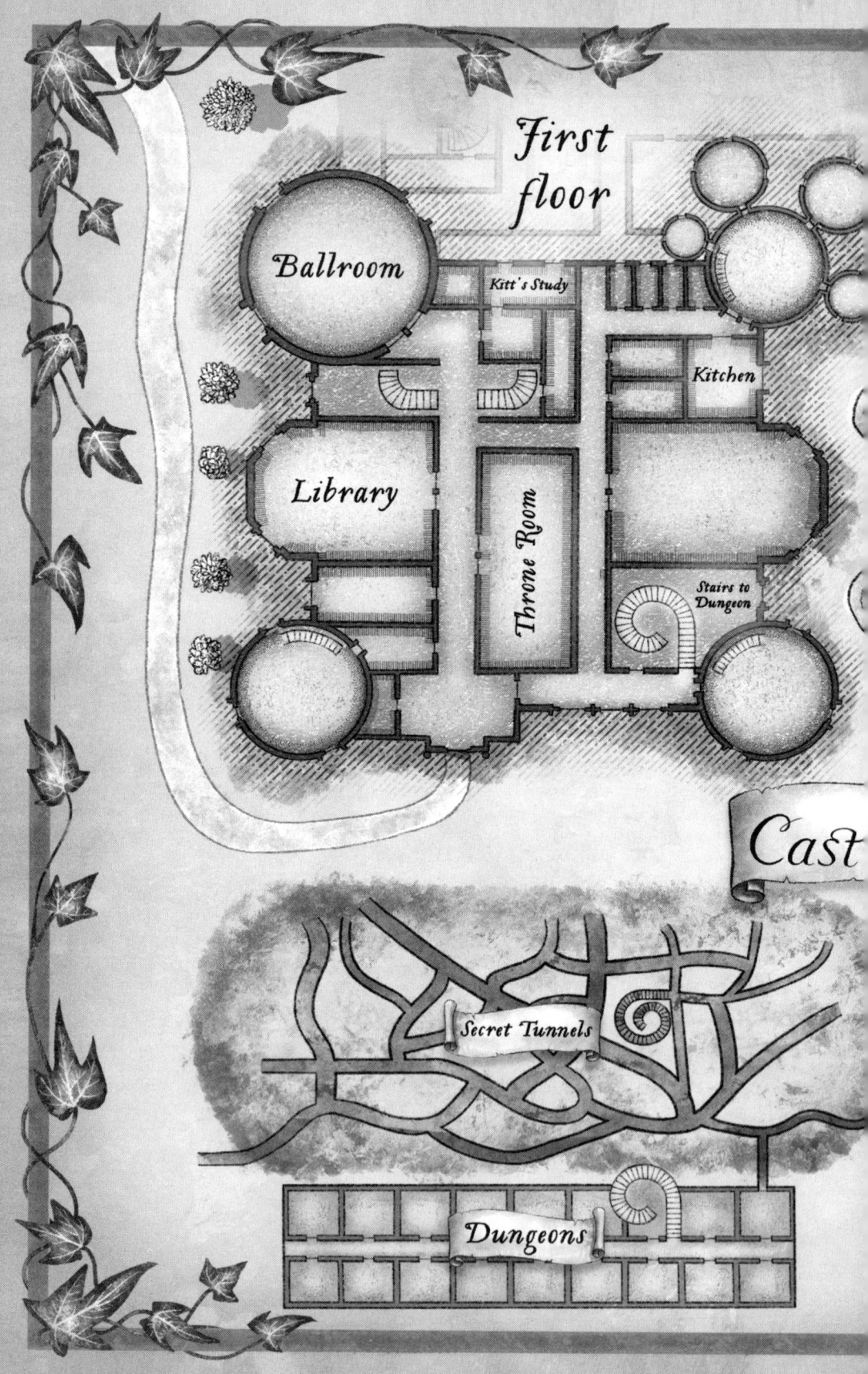

PROLOGUE
Mara

The dead struggle as though they have something left to live for.

This body is particularly heavy as it sputters at Death's heels. Though, not in the way that dragging a leaden corpse tends to exhaust a human. You see, Death is equipped with everything she needs to damn the dead. When she beckons for strength, it answers. When temptation is required of her, she dons beauty like armor. And when Death needs to live up to her ruthless name, she certainly does.

One would do well to remember this.

No, it is the weight of this man's soul that slows her steps. A darkness swirls around his still heart, coating the cold skin he wears with past sins as slippery as oil beneath Death's touch. Using as few fingers as possible (Death does not like to dirty

her hands), she drags the pleading man by his ankle across the murky swamp. He may be dead in the land of the living, but here, death is a kindness you earn. So his stiff body twists in the mud as he begs for mercy, filling his gaping mouth with inky sludge.

Death does not look back. She already knows what the face of duty looks like. For she is just as damned as the souls she retrieves.

A thick fog creeps across the decaying ground to crowd Death's path and choke the man she drags. Wading through the ominous vapor, Death pauses beneath a rotting tree to draw a deep breath. The stench of this man's stained soul is now mercifully stifled by the sea of fog he drowns beneath. Taking advantage of the peaceful moment, Death peers up at the bare branches clawing their way towards a perpetually gray sky. Gnarled trunks sprout from the muddy ground like bony fingers to point at the life beyond this glorified graveyard.

Unfazed by the eeriness of her birthplace (figuratively speaking, of course), Death weaves between the ashen trees with the thrashing soul in tow. Moss drips from each branch to slither over Death's shoulders and skim across her brow like a slippery veil. Like a runaway bride returned.

The Mors welcome home their own.

Dragging that sputtering soul through the cluster of skeletal trees, Death laughs as she parts a curtain of moss. They do love to gossip — the trees, that is. Or rather, the souls planted within them. Some hear only the whistling of wind through their branches, but those who know death firsthand will always recognize it in another's voice.

Bones crunch beneath Death's feet as she emerges from the cluster of equally brittle trees. The soul, with his ankle bruising between the delicate fingers of a deceptively alluring woman, cries out as a severed femur nicks his muddy skin (the bones were a bit much, Death could admit). Blood trickles from his forearm to smear the decaying ground, which greedily laps up the life it rarely tastes, bucking towards this soul as if it were an inflated lung. The man screams when the crumbling ground begins to breathe beneath him like the salivating creature it is.

'Not yet.' Death softly scolds the earth's ravenous appetite. Its responding rumble is meek below her feet while the soul at her heels continues its violent thrash. Drawing a long, blackened sword with her free hand, Death uses its soul-stained tip to nudge aside the several bones blocking her path (Death does not like to dirty her boots, either).

At the sight of such a sinister blade, now dripping with an inky vapor, the man screams again. 'Please! Please, let me go! I—!'

'There is no reason to shout.' Death's voice is smooth — perhaps even what one might consider to sound sincere. For the first time since stealing him from the living, she turns to look at the soul she drags. He is fascinatingly forgettable, she thinks as her dark eyes roam over his dull brown hair and muddied features. But he wears the face of fear, and that, however tedious, is familiar. 'No one can hear you,' she finishes simply.

The man blinks up at her in terror. 'B-but . . . you can hear me . . . ?'

Death allows herself a moment to pity this soul. 'I am not who you want answering your prayers.'

With that, she turns to continue tugging her captured soul to its doom. The tip of that inky sword hangs from her hand to drag across the dry ground, spitting sparks in her wake. The man sputters from behind, prompting her to say, 'Don't mind the bones. I put them here for show.'

'W-what?' the man chokes out.

'Humans have high expectations for death. For as much as everyone dreads it, they spend most of their life pondering the end of it, and just how terrible it will be.' Licking her lips, Death speaks what she often does – the truth. Death has no patience for decorum, so she finds that most words her tongue forms are frank. 'I didn't want to disappoint.'

Mercifully, the man stops his struggling. 'So the bones . . . aren't real?'

'What a silly question.' There is Death's charming bluntness. 'Especially because you already know the answer to it.'

The soul's cooperation is short-lived.

Sighing through her nose, Death gladly drops the man's ankle. Ashen trees loom overhead once again, and the soul blinks up at their mossy branches from a spot well-worn into the decaying earth. Death pulls a handkerchief from her cloak to wipe the grime of a sinful soul from her hands. 'You're free to go.'

The man sits up suddenly. Mud dribbles down his chin like the disbelief tumbling from his mouth. 'I . . . I am?'

'Well, you can lie there if you like.' Death shrugs a shoulder. This, of all things, makes the man flinch beneath her. Such a flippant gesture, as though she's donned the skin of a human that doesn't quite fit right, is chilling on a creature so fearsome. 'You are free to do whatever you like,' she says simply.

'But . . . what am I supposed to do?' the man asks hesitantly.

'Find a way out of the Mors.' Death takes a step back. 'Or don't.'

The soul scrambles to his feet before hurling questions at his captor. 'There is a way out? What am I supposed to look for? Will I get to go back home?'

Death answers to no man. Instead, she leaves him with a promise that most have spent an eternity clinging to. 'You are all alone here. Unless you find a way out.'

Then she turns, banishing the soul to solitude.

Yet he will never truly be alone. Not like she.

Lifting her gaze, Death is met with a sea of swarming souls. Like a writhing blanket, bodies drape every inch of the barren land. Every face is frantic, every soul searching for their freedom. They pass through one another, completely unaware of anything but the loneliness festering within them.

And Death cuts through them all – a scythe cleaving through shadows.

Glancing over a shoulder, she watches her fresh soul search the cracked earth for his escape. His eyes are alight with hope as he rakes through the mud, unaware of the dozens beside him doing the same.

Death looks away, dismayed.

They all dull eventually. Isolation eats at the mind, but still, those unable to accept their fate search for a way out of it. The constant drone of wailing souls is a lullaby Death steps in time to (they often tend to unknowingly harmonize with their sorrow). Weaving between the milling bodies, Death scrutinizes each soul, absently counting off the common ways in which the dead cope.

There is crying, of course. (This is the obvious reaction.) Then there are the souls who stare unseeingly at the dull sky above, having been here long enough to lack the energy to do much else. And finally, there are those who have searched every inch of the Mors for their freedom, only to have lost their sanity.

One soul in particular (Death knows each of her victims, and this woman has haunted the Mors for nearly a millennium) claws at a whispering tree.

'Let me in! Let me in! I know you're in there!'

Averting her gaze, Death strides past the howling woman to find refuge beneath a tree of her own. Its whisper is familiar, the soul within a friend. So Death sits at the tree's gnarled roots and leans her head against the ashy trunk. Shutting her eyes, she tugs on the fraying lifelines each human teeters upon. Death herself does not choose who to knock from their tightrope, only who to catch first once they have fallen.

This is her fate – escorting others to it.

Like an intricate spiderweb, countless lifelines stretch out within Death's mind. She toys with those that begin to fray – a woman nearly trampled by a rogue horse; a little boy contemplating popping a plump, poisonous berry into his mouth; a man with enemies lurking in a shadowed alley. But Death does not waste her time on possible danger or the prospect of demise. No, she searches for a life that is already slipping away; a soul that has lost their balance atop the tightrope.

A man flashes in Death's mind. His golden hair is disheveled above a pair of wild, green eyes. He is arguing, agitated, though his words are muffled.

But that is not what startles Death (little does, you see). It is the familiarity of his features, like a distant memory, that has her stilling.

Stern faces surround him, flashing in Death's mind before she feels this man's lifeline fray irreversibly.

He lifts a vial to his lips and swallows.

Fate sears through a once-strong strand, cutting this young life gruesomely short.

Death gasps. Something in her hollow chest burns.

This demise feels different. Personal. Intimate.

Taken aback, Death furrows her brow as she attempts to deepen her connection to him. Few humans have managed to intrigue her, certainly none that looked like him. Not in this lifetime, at least.

This man willingly tasted death, forfeited his future. And the Keeper of the Mors would like to know why.

She stands to her feet. Shakes her head. Even smiles slightly.

Death swore she would die before setting foot back in Ilya.

CHAPTER 1

Kitt

The Plague burns down my throat.

This is what pure power must taste like.

The Healers' protests grow muffled in my ears, mingling with the shouts of every encircling Scholar.

I watch as a wave of disbelief crashes over their blurry faces.

I ordered that they bring me this perfected dose.

Now it is they who must keep me alive.

Foolish, reckless, mad – I don't care.

I have great plans for Ilya.

I only need to evade Death.

CHAPTER 2

Mara

Life is much duller than it was when Death once possessed it.

This saddens her slightly. She was hoping to be impressed by mankind.

Alas, with a disapproving drawing of breath (it tastes of smoke and the decaying leaves crunching beneath her boots), Death follows the scent of a soul eager to meet her. Her lungs have no need for air, but some habits – a body reflexively drawing breath, desperate to provide its host with life – die hard. You see, Death takes it upon herself to appreciate the things humans fail to, and breathing is certainly a thankless phenomenon.

So, with damp air filling useless organs, Death strolls across the castle grounds with all the confidence of a royal.

There is a distant familiarity here, no matter the blandness that has now blanketed this kingdom. The trees are gnarled, bowing beneath the unforgivable hand of Time. Even the sky hanging above seems bleached of its usual vibrance as Death drags her fingers along the castle's chalky stones.

Yes, much duller than she remembers.

Guards pass in a lazy procession, ignorant to Death's watchful gaze. She doesn't mind their lack of recognition – or anyone else's, for that matter. In fact, she has grown to enjoy the quiet pocket from which she observes the living. Death is a demanding role, as one can imagine, but she finds the trivial troubles of mankind to be a delightful distraction.

A human fussing over a blemish on their skin. One begrudgingly eating a bowl of oats they believe is beneath them. Another arguing with their lover over a quite obvious misunderstanding.

Apparently, these are the things worth living for. And Death finds that most amusing. Her favorite pastime – between gathering souls and acquainting them with a maddening solitude – consists of what most would wrongly identify as spying. No, her acute observation is a manifestation of curiosity. Research to aid in her occupation. A passion for the mundane (humans) and the tragic (their tedious lives).

You see, Death is much more than her namesake. She is a lady, after all (that fact alone should be interesting enough). Can she not have hobbies?

Death takes her time roaming the countless castle corridors. She is in no rush – not like the living. Besides, there is hardly anything new to explore. Time has left this piece of the past perfectly intact. It's quite haunting, but not in the way Death can usually appreciate. You see, she does not enjoy having a tangible reminder of her greatest mistake.

Nestling into the folds of her cloak, Death weaves between the puddles of sunlight soaking the plush floor. That tugging in her chest grows stronger with each step, and she eagerly carves a path towards the soul at this tether's end. Because in all of Death's years, she has never known an Azer to so willingly part with their power.

Dying is hardly something kings do gracefully. For that very reason, Death so enjoys her time spent with royals. Even when looking up at her from the Mors' muddy floor, they still unflinchingly command. It's intriguing, watching a powerful human slowly recognize what they have become – nothing more than a stranded soul caught in Fate's web.

'With all due respect, Your Majesty, you do know that this is still insane?'

This polite disbelief drifts from the dim room that summons Death. The soul within calls to her, fraying beneath the weight of some irreparable decision. Her tie to this human runs deep, as though their veins are knotted together, hearts humming the same tune. Though the organ is long cold in Death's unmoving chest, it recognizes itself in the one that pumps borrowed time, mere steps away.

This soul is foolish enough to hope.

And a lifetime ago, so was Death.

'I'm aware,' responds a different male voice, this one far smoother. He doesn't sound like a man who wants to die. 'But it needs to be done. Can I count on you?'

Death pauses in the hallway, awaiting her entrance and the confrontation of her curiosity. There is hardly any need to startle the dying soul in front of another. She is not a monster, after all. Her connection to this man allows physical contact, the ability to behold. But Death is unused to being seen by the somewhat living. This oddity will be a first for the both of them.

'Yes, Your Majesty.' It's the first voice. Death notes that it sounds like he is accustomed to curving each sentence into something comedic, as though he can hardly take himself seriously. 'You can count on me. I only hope I, uh, live to tell the tale.'

This comment, combined with that incessant curiosity, has Death stretching a strand of her power towards the man. His soul is not marked for the Mors. In fact, she can see his sprawling lifeline clearly – it is long, and happier than most.

Death sighs. For the umpteenth time over the decades, she marvels at the self-importance of humans. Every soul believes they are worthy of being stalked by Death. But you see, she is a busy woman. One who doesn't waste her time on a man's paranoia of her possible presence.

If you wish to grab Death's attention, then die.

'Let's hope Blair's on her best behavior.' It's that steady voice again. 'I'll be here if you need anything.'

There is a rustling of fabric before a shadow curls across the carpet. A man, dressed in a blinding ensemble of white, halts in the doorframe. His masked face turns back towards the king. 'Not that it matters coming from me, but I think it's really great what you're doing for the kingdom. And Calum is a good man – I hope to help you both in any way I can.'

How sincere, Death thinks. Though, she sees no point in speaking otherwise.

Death appreciates – expects, really – words that carry weight behind them. The kind capable of welling eyes and softening even the stoniest of hearts. It's one of the few things humans do right – feeling.

'Thank you, Lenny,' the king returns softly. Death thinks he sounds hesitant. She thinks a lot of things, most of them all at once but never portrayed on her placid features. She carries herself with a stoic sort of practiced professionalism.

Death is quite attentive for someone her age.

This *Lenny* strolls into the hallway with a fading smile. Though, he looks rather anxious – an expression that is likely foreign on his freckled face. Death eyes him closely, tracing the coils of red hair that bounce with each of his lanky strides. So when his head suddenly swivels in her direction, she is startled half to death (as the living like to say, though it's a gross exaggeration used without her consent).

Unsurety creases Lenny's brow. Then his warm eyes collide with Death's frigid gaze.

She is pinned to the wall like a carcass on display. After living (proverbially, of course) in the shadows for decades, unseen and unburdened by identity, she is suddenly beheld. This boy who smells of starch — a point Death feels cannot go unnoticed — is the first to acknowledge her presence.

She is not sure what to make of this.

Peering beyond this physical realm, she studies his soul. It is like drawing back a curtain to find the next layer of one's being behind. And this soul is bright — glowing with a yellow sheen. Death predicted as much.

Lenny looks away, shaking his head. 'Shit,' he mumbles. 'I really am paranoid.'

With that declaration of defeat, he sets off down the hall once again.

Death stares longingly at his retreating form. Then at the wall separating her from that flickering, blue soul within the study.

Her foot taps a steady beat against the floor. On occasion, she pretends the rhythm belongs to her heart. It provides some semblance of comfort, though she doesn't care to question why.

After much deliberation, Death follows the lingering scent of starch through the castle. She warrants this diversion because no living being has ever sensed her presence.

The mystery of this starchy man is worth Death's valuable

time. Besides, the king will still be dying when she returns.

Death is rather blunt. Sensitivity is hardly in her job description.

The guard leads her out into the training yard, where his white attire only further blinds in the streaming sunlight. He treads carefully towards a young woman who hogs the little shade offered by a generous tree. She is sprawled atop the soft grass, strands of striking lilac hair clinging to her slick brow.

It looks as though she has been exercising. What an unappealing use of life.

The woman frowns at the swelling sound of rustling fabric. Then she scowls when it speaks.

'Wow, you're actually sweating. Maybe you are human.'

Death finds this introduction fascinating. Perhaps she can collect some enticing gossip to share with the trees back home.

The young lady's eyes fly open. Then she promptly sweeps her scrutiny over him. 'All that starch much be getting to your head. I don't think you know who you're talking to.'

(Death feels strangely validated by her acknowledgment of such an excessive scent. Moments like these make her grateful for the ability to cease breathing.)

That is all the woman deigns to say before settling back into the bed of grass and letting her eyes drift closed. She seems to bask in the quiet stillness, lacing fingers over her abdomen in contentment.

'So, uh, still here.'

Death watches as the woman lifts herself into a sitting position, huffing all the while. 'Did I not imply that you should be walking away right now?' Her voice is impressively condescending.

'Trust me—' Lenny lifts his hands in mock surrender '—I would. But unfortunately for the both of us, I can't.'

'Here.' That alluring hair hardly softens this woman's sharp features. Her smile is mocking. 'Allow me to help.'

The guard's boots leave the ground suddenly, and he practically squeals. 'The king! I'm here on behalf of the king!'

So this is the Blair who has men fearing for their lives. She is powerful – that much is obvious. But like every other Elite, she has done nothing to deserve this strength. It is borrowed. Stolen.

Death takes a seat on the grass, preparing for the show. Though, to her dismay, it doesn't last long. The Tele – Death so enjoys these silly titles – stands to her feet before setting the guard on his own. Now reunited with the ground, Lenny runs a gloved hand down his face and fights to find his composure.

There is not an ounce of disdain withheld from Blair's expression. 'You were a foot off the ground.' A slow blink. 'If that.'

'Yes, and I was overcome with empathy for those taller than me,' Lenny muses.

Both Death and Blair simply stare at him, thoroughly unimpressed.

He blinks those brown eyes behind that mask, the same ones that unknowingly met Death's. Flatly, he adds, 'I'm joking.'

'Right. Now would you like me to explain why I didn't laugh?'

'Let me guess.' The guard's voice is falsely cheerful. 'You don't know how?'

Death's gaze flicks between them.

'No, because laughter typically accompanies something that is *funny*,' Blair retorts with a well-practiced pout.

Lenny sighs in defeat. 'All right, let's just get this over with.' He claps his gloved hands together, as if to brace himself against the words leaving his lips. 'Paedyn is back.'

Blair swallows swiftly. Very watchful, Death. 'And? Why would I care that the traitor has been caught?'

'Because the king has plans for her. Plans that keep her alive to help Ilya.'

'Again,' the temperamental Tele bites out, 'why does this concern me?'

Impulsively, the guard pulls that mask from his face to display an additional dozen freckles. His nose is straight. Jaw strong. Eyes earnest. Death recognizes his need for Blair to see the emotion etched into his features. He is desperate to bridge an honest connection between them.

How very human.

Blair takes a wary step back. Death, disconcerted, feels the urge to do the same.

She can appreciate a baring of one's emotions, an outright invitation for connection. But Death has earned the right to numbness. She wishes not for unsolicited feelings and the repercussions of them. So, sitting this close to such sentiment makes her tense.

'You know what Paedyn will try to do to you,' Lenny murmurs.

'Yes.' Brown eyes roll behind several strands of lilac hair. 'The key word there is "try".'

Death is thoroughly enthralled. The afterlife is hardly this dramatic.

'Paedyn won't stop.' There is an urgency in the guard's gaze. 'Especially if you are sharing the same castle. And the king needs to keep you safe.'

'The Slummer is a traitor,' Blair spits. It's been a lifetime since Death has heard that insult. 'Why would she be living lavishly in the castle with—?'

'You will find out soon enough,' Lenny interrupts before swallowing thickly. 'All you need to know now is that I . . . I am to be your personal guard. To protect you from Paedyn.'

A moment of stifling silence passes between them.

Then, a startling cackle bellows from Blair. 'Now that . . .' She snorts. '*That* was a joke.'

The guard lets out a weak, uncomfortable laugh. 'Oh, you are really not going to find this funny when you realize I'm serious.'

Death considers cracking a smile at such captivating entertainment. She does not, of course. Those are saved for special occasions.

Blair takes a slow step forward, her voice drenched in ice. 'You? Protect me? From Paedyn Gray?'

'Whoa.' Lenny lifts his hands again. 'Let's not . . . throw the messenger through the air with your mind, okay? I'm just doing as I'm told.'

The Tele does look rather frightening in this moment. More so than most find Death to be. But that doesn't bother the Mother of the Mors – she quite likes to be underestimated. Earning a look of terror from a man is all the more rewarding that way.

No, Death isn't a monster. She's just bored.

'And who, exactly, told you this?' Blair snaps.

'Like I said, it was—'

The Tele's arm is suddenly outstretched, lifting Lenny from the ground yet again. 'Was it the sergeant?'

He squirms in her mental grip, growing pale. 'Sergeant?' His voice cracks. 'Your father's a general, not—'

'Someone had to convince the king I needed protection from an Ordinary,' Blair seethes. 'This is her doing. This is her attempt to embarrass me.'

Death's head swivels between them.

'What? Look,' the guard pants, 'I have no idea what you're talking about. The king doesn't want her trying to fight you — that's all. And he thinks I'm the best person to put between the two of you, because Pae won't hurt me to get to her best friend's killer.'

An indirect mention of Death. This makes her feel strangely included in the conversation.

Blair's wrathful gaze grows distant. She wears the look of someone revisiting a memory, a pivotal point in time. Death tilts her head, as she often does when one manages to intrigue her. For she recognizes, more intimately than most, the face of regret.

The Tele's power (still comical, these entitlements) falters, reuniting Lenny with the ground he so craves. Little surprises Death in her old age — wonderment is due to a lack of experience, you see. But when the guard strides towards Blair, even Death could not have predicted this sudden spur of boldness.

He halts mere inches from the king's assignment, their bodies close.

Blair lifts her chin, singeing him with a scathing look.

Lenny does his best to mirror her sentiment.

Death is certain the trees will never believe her.

The anger on the guard's face looks foreign, as though he hardly knows how to express the emotion. 'Believe it or not—' he laughs humorlessly '—there is nothing I'd like less than spending time with you. But the king is ordering you to remain in your room until he says otherwise, and because of my closeness to Paedyn, I'm unlucky enough to guard you from her.'

Impossibly, Blair's gaze narrows further. 'You were her assigned Imperial.'

Death files the word away for future use. She hadn't realized guards now require a fancier title. Ilya so loves to invent importance.

Lenny nods, confirming the Tele's statement.

Calmly – worryingly so – Blair asks, 'And what is your power?'

'That's your first question?' The *Imperial* shakes his head (it is a fun word, Death supposes). 'Not, I don't know, what my name is, or—'

'I don't give a damn what your name is, gingersnap,' Blair taunts. 'What is your power?'

Lenny sighs. 'I'm a Hyper.'

'A Hyper . . .' Her echo of disbelief is followed by a scoff. 'Well, it's a good thing I don't actually need protection from an Ordinary, otherwise, I'd be dead.'

Death feels a bit left out now. She is hardly well-versed in Elite abilities, though power is familiar, relative. No, it's the accompanying pomposity that is foreign to Death. Such strength is not for humans to name.

'Hilarious.' Lenny's tone suggests otherwise. 'Now, let's get you to your room before—'

'How do I know you're not just saying all of this?' Blair snaps.

The Imperial she so endearingly deemed 'gingersnap' gestures to himself in exasperation. 'Do I look like I'm enjoying this?'

Blair bristles, but her snide tone hardly falters. 'Well, then, maybe I should just put you out of your misery, hmm?'

Death inches closer when the Tele lifts a hand, readying to rain down her (this possession is used loosely) power on the Imperial. But Lenny only tilts his head, ever so slightly. He seems to be intrigued by something. Death's own curiosity is reflected within his gaze. 'No . . .' the alleged Hyper says slowly. 'You don't want to kill me.'

Hmm.

Death will have to disagree. It seems, to the adept embodiment of demise, that the Tele has every intention of ridding herself of him. But humans are confusing creatures. Perhaps Death has misread the situation (doubtful, but she isn't opposed to being proven wrong).

Blair opens her mouth, expecting words to form.

Her declared gingersnap only shrugs. 'Maybe you really are human.'

Death ponders this quietly, stoically — as she does most things. (Though, she could just as easily skip alongside a strolling pair of lovers, shed a tear for the souls she collects, laugh at the punchline of an overheard joke. But Death does not see the point in parading her emotions, for there is no one to partake in them with her. It is better to feel nothing than it is to feel everything alone.) Is this what makes one human, the valuing of another life? The acknowledgment of worth, of beauty, of something to live for? Death can no longer remember.

Proof of Blair's humanity is only a glimpse away for a creature as powerful as Death. Curiously, she parts that spiritual curtain, peeking behind it into a different plane entirely. Lenny's soul glows golden while Blair's swirls a murky green.

Death blinks.

She might have even gasped, though no one bore witness to prove it.

Slowly, Death stands to her feet. Walks a tight perimeter around the glowering pair. No longer listens to a word they are saying.

There is nothing at all but this moment in which two souls — opposite in every way — reach for each other.

Death steps closer still to the phenomenon. If she had any need for breath, it would tickle their skin with her proximity. Her gaze narrows on the stretching strands of each soul. They ebb and flow like a timid tide, emerald meeting gold in a moment long predestined.

Their souls aren't quite enlaced like the fate of lovers, but not entirely detached like those destined to remain strangers.

They are something else entirely. A bond of their choosing.

Death grows as still as her name implies.

It's not their mingling of souls that startles her — no, she is quite familiar with the concept. These two mortals, she determines, could not be more wrong for each other. Because Death has witnessed – *suffered* – the intertwining of souls. This couldn't possibly be something so sacred.

For that reason, Death decides to see what becomes of these indecisive souls. She could almost laugh at their unfortunate pairing. Fate certainly has a sense of humor, drawing them together.

If nothing else, this will be, undoubtedly, entertaining.

'. . . strangle you in your sleep,' Blair is threatening when Death retakes her seat with a sigh. It seems the Tele has conceded to the king's orders, albeit furiously.

Lenny smiles, and it's impressively void of all emotion. 'That would be a kindness, which means you won't actually do it.'

Death leans back on her palms, watching them bicker.

If those truly meant for each other could not survive the fateful intertwining of their souls, she thinks bitterly, these two will surely tear each other apart.

She is not heartless, Death.

Not quite.

The broken organ just no longer beats.

CHAPTER 3

Kitt

My eyes trace his neat handwriting for the hundredth time.

I've memorized Father's final farewell, and the truth within it taunts me. I see the sentences when I close my eyes, taste the string of syllables on my tongue.

My tired gaze glides down the inky page to that staggering secret.

As Ilya's king, you now guard her secrets. And just as my father did for me, I leave behind the truth. The Plague that gifted us our powers was no accident. It was created to strengthen our kingdom, and it did just that — though, not in the way Favian Azer intended.

Carelessly, I shove the letter back into the drawer where I found it.

But I do not need the words before me. Father's voice still echoes in my mind.

'No one but the court Scholars and Healers know of this – and it will remain that way. This power is for Ilya alone. We will never again be a weak kingdom. And if I am unable to rid us of the remaining Ordinaries, you will continue my work for me. They are a defect of the unfinished Plague, a disease that must be cleansed from our legacy.'

I shake my head at Father's demand for the hundredth time.

What a waste of the power we possess. What a waste of all those years I spent believing Father was doing something great – something worth the constant lack of approval.

I drum my fingers against the chipped desk, my heart pounding in time.

That was his pivotal plan? Ridding Ilya of some cowering Ordinaries was all the fearsome Edric Azer could devise?

A knock at the study door scares off my growing agitation. I clear my throat. 'Come in.'

Scholars parade solemnly into the study, their procession followed by an equally grim filing of Healers. They surround my desk stiffly, some shuffling parchment while others ready various vials of ominous herbs. I dread this daily ambush, though it is entirely my doing.

The head court Healer greets me with a curt 'Your Majesty.'

It's odd, knowing that the man who healed every one of Kai's and my wounds growing up has been entrusted with the truth of our Plague. I nod at the weathered Healer. 'How are you, Eli?'

His cold fingers begin their routine prodding at my throat. 'Well, I'm still very displeased with you, my young King.'

I can't help but smile at his boldness. 'I appreciate the honesty.'

'I'm old,' he states. 'I'm allowed to say whatever I like. It's quite nice, actually.'

He gestures for me to stand while rattling off his observations for the other Healers to document. Then his palms are on my back, feeling each breath I take. A tingling sensation travels up my spine as he seeps some of his power into me.

Ten minutes pass, and still, I stand there beneath the Healer's icy hands. Just as I have every day since swallowing a dose of the Plague three days ago.

'Drink this,' Eli orders, offering me a murky vial.

I stare skeptically at the brown liquid. 'You demanded I not take the Plague, but this . . . this you want me to ingest?'

'You told us to keep you alive.' The Healer doesn't bother masking his irritation. 'Even knowing another dose of the Plague might be fatal to an Elite, you took it before I had the chance to pin you down myself.' The old man wags a finger in my face, unafraid of the crown currently sitting on my head. 'So, yes, you will drink this tincture, because my power can't help you now. We're not sure if anything can.'

For a brief moment, I wonder if I should reprimand the brazen Healer. It's what my father would do, after all. He would demand respect, no matter how undeserving of it he was.

But I am not my father.

I nod and lift the vial to my lips.

I will be so much greater.

The tonic burns down my throat, so putrid I fear it will find its way back up. I brace a hand against the back of my chair and cough violently. 'Wow,' I croak. 'That was . . . something.'

'Let's hope it was something.' Eli shuffles around the desk to peek at a Healer's notes. 'We have no idea what to do with you.'

'I know,' I say distantly. 'I was aware of the risks.'

Memory of that night flashes in my mind — Healers arguing about the danger; Scholars begging to hoard our power. I had heard their pleas a dozen times before, ever since I found my father's letter and demanded a meeting with those who knew the truth of our power. But I had already made up my mind.

Eli's voice is hushed. 'And if you live? Become the strongest Elite?' His white brows knit together. 'You can't go through with it.'

'I am your king,' I say sternly. All that ruthlessness Father demanded of me seeps into the words. 'You will fall into place, or I will make you.'

Eli stares at me for a long moment, perhaps reminiscing on a time when I was weak and malleable. Then, with a soft 'Yes, my King,' he steps back into line with his fellow Healers.

'Your Majesty?'

My gaze flicks to a Scholar still scribbling on his parchment. I stifle my sigh. 'No, I don't have any symptoms.'

'No headaches?' he pries, reminiscent of the past few days. 'Any tightness in your chest? Coughing? Memory loss?'

'It's been three days,' I counter. 'I feel perfectly fine. Now, if you're done poking at me—' I gesture to the parchment scattered across my desk '—I have work to do.'

Heads bob around the room with each begrudging bow. I watch the cluster of Elites begin filing from my study, the head Healer lagging behind. Eli turns then, wearing a look of defeat. 'May the Plague spare you, my young King.'

His words hang in the air long after I watch him leave. Sighing into the stillness I'm now left with, I begin shuffling the assortment of paper on my desk.

A slight chill slithers down my spine.

I clear my throat and vaguely wonder if I've left the window open.

'What is this work you have to do?'

I startle at the soft voice, then at the stranger it comes from.

A woman stares at me from beside the crackling fireplace, her hair the color of a stolen ember. I blink – once, twice – because I'm certain she's a figment of my imagination. Perhaps the Plague really is getting to me. Surely nothing can be this magnificent.

Yet, there she stands, brown eyes pinning me to the spot.

This is the most beautiful woman I've ever seen, and all I can manage is a blurted 'What are you doing in here?'

The placid look on her perfect features never budges. 'Indulging my morbid curiosity.'

'Are you one of the Healers?' I shake my head. 'I think I would have remembered.'

'What makes you think I'm not a Scholar?'

She doesn't pose the question in that sly way Paedyn might have, nor does she feign offense like Andy so enjoys. No, the words are genuine, her tone betraying intrigue.

Clearing my throat, I attempt a touch of humor. 'You don't seem entirely dull.'

'Hmm.' It's not a laugh, but rather, the sound of someone making an observation. 'So what is it you're working on?'

'Oh.' I'm still struggling to form a coherent thought. 'Kingly matters, mostly. But some . . . personal.'

'I won't pry like the Scholars,' she says simply.

I brace my hands on the desk, chuckling softly. 'In truth, it's nice to speak with someone. My thoughts are shared only with the letters I write. It's . . .' I rub at the back of my neck. 'It's how I clear my head.'

She laces thin fingers in front of the black garb draping her body. 'Did you tell those letters why you wished to take a Plague you know nothing about?'

'Know nothing about?' I laugh again despite myself. 'I know

more now than I ever have. I know how the Scholars created it a century ago to strengthen our army against invasions. Then the Plague spread, accidentally or not, through Ilya.' My fingers drum against the strewn parchment. 'That is more than the kingdom knows. They don't like to think on the tragedy, only what it gave us.'

She huffs sharply, and the sound slightly resembles a laugh. 'Is that what they told you?'

'What else would they tell me?' I venture slowly.

'Maybe how those great Scholars created this *Plague* a hundred years ago.'

My voice dips into something earnest. I lean on my elbows, peering over the desk at her. 'Do you know something your fellow Healers do not?'

'It is not difficult to know more than men.'

The lack of humor in her voice makes me smile. 'Well, there are woman Healers. You are proof of that.'

Her stoic features seem to flinch with a sudden emotion. Then she nods, ever so slightly.

There is something so strangely intriguing about this woman. Her voice is dull, and yet, it seems she only bothers uttering words worth her breath. 'I haven't thought to ask for specifics,' I finally admit. 'I'm sure it's all too complex for me to comprehend.'

'Hmm.' There is that almost-laugh again. 'I'm sure it is.'

Her words drift into the space between us before a swelling

silence swallows them. Firelight flickers against her auburn hair as she stands across my study, absurdly still yet effortlessly relaxed.

'I did tell the letters.'

I'm not sure why I say it, but the soft words are suddenly spilling from my mouth.

The stranger says nothing, but those deep brown eyes voice her intrigue.

'I told the letters why I took the Plague,' I clarify. 'I ordered a perfected dose be brought to me, because I need to save the Elites from going extinct. Our power has dwindled over time, fevers manage to kill us every year, which I now know is because the Plague wasn't ready to be released. But the Scholars have refined what was spread a century ago.'

A shadow of amusement falls over her face.

'So I'm seeing what will happen to an Elite who takes another dose,' I continue firmly. 'Then I will strengthen every kingdom with the Plague.'

She considers this for a moment. 'But you didn't need to be the Elite who risked their life to test a theory.'

'I'm the king,' I say simply. 'These are my plans for the kingdom. It was only right I took the Plague.'

'Hmm.'

I raise my brows incredulously. 'What?'

Her shoulders lift slightly before dropping. It is the first bit of movement I've seen from her. 'You just don't seem like the type to lie.'

'Oh,' I chuckle, 'you think I'm lying?'

'I think your motives weren't entirely selfless,' she counters evenly.

'Fine.' I swallow my pride before spitting out the words. 'My father always thought I was weak. He would tell me every day. Maybe part of me wanted another dose so I would become so much stronger than he ever was.' I hold her unwavering stare. 'Just like I want to be so much greater.'

Her dark eyes flick over me. 'Hmm. You have enough of this Plague to infect the other kingdoms?'

'It doesn't take much,' I assure. 'Undiluted, we have about a vial of the dark liquid. But the dosage has been perfected over the century. You only need a few drops, or an object coated in the substance.'

She doesn't miss a beat. 'And what happens when you don't live to rule over these Elite cities like you hoped?'

'When?' I laugh tightly. 'At least give me a chance to survive.'

'You did have a chance,' the stranger says plainly. 'A chance at a long life, in fact. But you chose the prospect of power.'

I shake my head at her. 'You certainly are a Healer. You sound just like the rest of them.' My fingers fidget with the paper pooling on my desk, if only to give myself something to do. 'But I feel fine. I will *be* fine. I'm sure of it.'

'No born Elite has ever taken this Plague. And it won't be kind to you – not again.' She tilts her head at me. The perplexed look on her face is the most emotion those placid features have allowed thus far. 'How you meet your fate will be a mystery. Even to me.'

I tilt my head right back. 'You are quite morbid, aren't you?'

Her eyes brighten with a flicker of amusement. 'You have no idea.'

'What is your name?' The question springs from my tongue after sitting at the tip of it for so long.

She strides towards the door, seemingly struggling to offer me an answer. Then, hushed and hesitant, the stranger reveals herself.

'Mara.'

CHAPTER 4
Mara

The Imperial is now banished to the corner of Blair's room. Generously supplied with three feet of floor to stand on, Lenny leans against the wall, glowering at his assignment over the barricade of furniture she has stacked around him. A desk teeters beneath the weight of a massive chest, while a dresser slumps against a vanity piled high with books. All it took was a thought, it seems, and the very room obeyed this Tele's command to compile a cage.

Death quite likes the dramatics of it all. Amid her obligation to deliver souls to the Mors (the joys of an eternal occupation), Mara has spent much of her time stalking this pair of begrudging souls. While it was the king who initially coaxed her from the Mors, these two bickering beings have managed to make Ilya all the more tolerable.

Death circles the room, cloak slithering along the floorboards while a smile threatens her lips.

They are doomed for each other.

'This is how you thank me after guarding your door all day?'

For the dozenth time, Lenny attempts to capture the attention of a lounging Blair. Propped on an elbow and perfectly unbothered, she flips the page of her book atop the only piece of furniture not currently crowding her prisoner. The sprawling bed is draped with a plum quilt and littered with pillows (they are rather soft – Death checked). So, it is understandable why Blair has yet to move from its plush embrace since Lenny escorted her here this morning.

Mara, however, cannot afford to rest – though it isn't required of the dead anyway. Juggling her curiosity between three living souls, along with the collection of countless deceased ones, is undoubtedly demanding. She left the conflicted humans to bicker in the training yard (see, Death can occasionally respect one's privacy) to, at last, make the king's acquaintance.

She has not stopped thinking about their conversation since, nor the way his green gaze crinkles with sincerity – but Mara would never admit such nonsense. The king is clearly a hopeful fool – dangerously so – who took a dose of this *Plague* he does not understand. There is no such thing as a perfected portion of raw power. Nothing so formidable can be controlled. Death knows this firsthand.

He will die. And Death will deliver his soul to the Mors.

Decidedly, she thinks no more on any of this. Not on the king's futile determination to live or the difficulty with which Mara remembered her name. It has been a lifetime since she needed to utter such intimacy. But Death did so as a parting gift to the king. He will not be around much longer to utter it – but Mara will be there the last time he does. She wishes to witness his final breath and every one between. Regrettably, her intrigue for the young man has only grown.

Perhaps Death will call Ilya home again, while she observes these three souls, if only for a little while.

'All right, that's it.' Lenny shoves off the wall, steps forward, and fills the final foot of space he has. 'I'm going through your stuff.'

It's an enticing endeavor that draws Mara closer. She leans over the barricade, watching the Imperial pull open a desk drawer and peer down at the cluttered mess inside. Death inches near the Hyper (she still has yet to discern what that pinch of power entails) with a buzzing sort of hesitancy. He has failed to notice her presence once more, so Mara simultaneously awaits and opposes the prospect of stealing his attention.

'Okay, well, clearly organization isn't your thing,' Lenny mumbles. 'Nor is kindness. Or refraining from taking prisoners.'

He digs through the mess of miscellaneous writing utensils and scraps of paper until—

'Hey, I didn't think you owned anything fun,' he huffs in disbelief before pulling a purple ball from the drawer. He bounces it on the little floor before him, watching it obediently return to his hand. 'This elicits too much joy – it couldn't possibly be yours. Did your last prisoner put it here?'

Death may actually find this Imperial to be funny.

Another bounce of his new toy. 'Plagues, you do like purple, don't you—?'

This time, the ball comes flying towards his face.

Lenny curses when it collides with his nose. Then, it promptly flees his presence, having been summoned into Blair's awaiting palm. She looks up with a slight pout, a sheet of lilac hair slipping over her shoulder. 'Keep talking, gingersnap. Your corner will only get smaller.'

(Death cannot decide whether she admires or animatedly dislikes this woman. Though, this is a common predicament when it comes to humans.)

Furniture scrapes against the wooden floor when Blair inches it towards the Imperial with her mind. Death leans over the tightening barricade to note that the satchel at his feet now occupies half the remaining standing space. Lenny simply tips his head against the wall in defeat. 'I only came in here to discuss our sleeping arrangements and you—'

'Provided a solution,' Blair finishes smugly. 'You may sleep there.'

Mara might feel bad for the Imperial. He laughs helplessly.

'Sleep here? In the three – I'm sorry – now two and a half feet of floor?'

The Tele snaps her book shut. It seems she finds another's distress to be bothersome. Death knows the feeling. 'You could always go sleep in your own room, Imperial. I'm not keeping you here.'

He gestures to the precarious barrier. 'You kind of are.'

'Don't try to be smart, gingersnap,' Blair huffs. 'You're not capable of it.'

Sighing, Lenny braces his arms against the dresser. Death does the same. The action feels quite human, and yet, she doesn't wish to rearrange her limbs.

'Look,' the Imperial grumbles, 'we have been over this. The king ordered me to guard you at all times, so that includes sleeping in this room with you. I would much rather be in the Imperials' quarters.' For good measure, he emphasizes with an earnest 'Trust me.'

But it is too late. Blair is already blissfully ignoring him once again.

Yes, never a dull moment with these two.

Mumbling curses at her, Lenny begins rifling through that desk drawer once again. A crinkled piece of parchment and broken charcoal are quickly scavenged from the clutter and set atop the dresser. Mara moves aside, adjusting her stance. The Imperial pays her no attention.

(This disappoints her. She's not entirely sure why.)

Lenny scribbles a hasty message onto the yellowed paper before folding it into a crude sort of glider. Death considers his creation with a healthy skepticism. Then, shutting one eye, he aims for Blair's face before letting the note fly.

She practically growls when the paper's folded point sails into her forehead. 'Would you like to be buried *beneath* the pile of furniture?'

'At least read the note first,' Lenny says, offended.

Death strides behind the bed, hovering over Blair's shoulder as she unfurls the parchment with a huff.

> Free me
> My feet are going numb
> I'll bring back sticky buns, you Tele tyrant

An interesting tactic, Mara thinks.

Blair simply stares at the note, unimpressed. 'This was your big offer?'

'Sticky buns are in high demand.'

'Well, they shouldn't be.' The Tele Tyrant crumbles the paper in her hand. 'They are mediocre, at best.'

'I'm sorry?' Lenny scoffs in disbelief. 'Mediocre? There really is no joy in your heart, is there?'

He poses a good question. Death looks to Blair, awaiting her answer.

'Fine.'

The furniture shifts, scraping against the floor in retreat. A clear pathway from the crowded corner presents itself, though Mara and the Imperial find her sudden compliance surprising. 'Fine, what? You're letting me go?' Lenny pries skeptically.

The Tele turns up her nose at him. 'Go find me sticky buns that aren't mediocre.'

'Oh, Gail's are anything but.'

'I'll be the judge of that.' Blair grins, displaying sharp canines. 'Now shoo.'

They spar, verbally, for a bit longer before Lenny finally slips from the room, locking the door behind. Death follows, her boredom a compass that points to this being an entertaining experience. The halls are crowded with scurrying servants and lined with an abundance of starchy Imperials. Lenny straightens, ever so slightly, in their presence. It seems to Mara that he quite likes his position here in the palace, perhaps because it makes him feel powerful. And strength is precisely what Blair insinuated he lacked.

Of course, this is just an observation on Death's part. Though, she prides herself on rarely being wrong. You can conceal nothing when dead, and the mother of such a state has grown rather good at seeing through the living.

Mara realizes, upon stepping into the stuffy kitchen, she could do with never revisiting. It is crowded and hot and if she weren't already very much dead, it might feel as though she were dying.

Everything is sticky — the air included. Death does not do sticky.

Lenny's visit with Gail is blessedly brief, though she is hesitant to hand over a pair of coveted sticky buns. But upon hearing of Blair Archer's (some dubious snooping yielded her full name) demand, the cook huffs out a laugh that has pink blossoming beneath her flour-stained cheeks. 'Oh, she won't like these, honey,' Gail informs. 'Somethin' about my pairing of spices.'

This doesn't seem to mean much to Lenny — he is a man, after all. They tend to lack the blissful gift of pondering for mere sport. But Death, a woman who yearns to find meaning in everything, wonders what connection the Tele has to this cook.

Mercifully, a swarm of servants shoves Lenny out into the hall, his palms occupied with glistening dough. The trek back to his cage is blamelessly begrudging. Falling behind the Imperial's stiff strides, Death stares at the starry sky blanketing Ilya beyond the wall of windows that adorns each hallway. Her first day back in this kingdom is coming to a close.

Mara, tapping her foot before the locked door they have returned to, watches her escort fumble hopelessly for the key within one of his many uniform pockets. Fortunately for Lenny, he pulls the sculpted iron from its starchy confines before Death's eye can start twitching. Nothing good ever follows a physical sign of her agitation.

'Okay, I'm gonna watch you eat this, because there is no

way you taste something this delicious and still manage to scowl at me—'

The Imperial steps into the room, only to stare blankly at the empty bed.

Hmm.

Death folds her arms.

This is certainly an unexpected development.

Lenny's eyes dart frantically around the space, finding every piece of furniture back in its rightful place. Chest, dresser, desk, vanity – now hugging their respective walls. The stone fireplace sits opposite the rumpled bed, framed with two draping tapestries.

'Blair?' the Imperial calls futilely.

He is met with no condescending response.

The Tele is gone.

Death's placidity, too, has vanished.

She smiles.

CHAPTER 5
Mara

Death is in no rush.

This is a concept that the living struggle to grasp. No, Mara is not stalking souls, awaiting their demise. She quite enjoys the slow moments, actually.

Wandering the slums of Ilya provides Death with plenty of time to ponder. She accompanied a very peeved Lenny from the castle, treading the long path right alongside him. Of course, Mara can step between planes and appear beside any soul (unbeknownst to them) of her choosing, but not tonight. Tonight she will spend time with herself.

When Death grew tired of struggling to keep up with the Imperial's long strides, she abandoned him to wander the slums. Now she weaves between crumbling buildings, lifting the hem of her cloak to dodge murky puddles. Despite the

late hour, Loot remains alive within the shadows. These self-proclaimed Elites scatter the market street, content to bask in the moonlight. They converse in clumps and play cards beneath the starry sky.

Some things never change, it seems.

(If she were more than a mere shadow in this realm, she might have dealt herself into the next hand. Mara is no stranger to Ilya's gambling games.)

Pointedly avoiding a nearby street (certain memories are best left buried), Mara continues her leisurely stroll down Loot. There is a contagious sort of freedom that resides here, as though one could be anything beneath Ilya's night sky. Perhaps even alive.

'. . . seen a woman with purple hair? She probably had a bitchy sort of look on her face?'

Death knows that voice. It drifts from a nearby alley, spouting descriptions that repeatedly include the use of 'condescending.' Mara spots the Imperial – his uniform is a beacon in the moonlight – striding from the cluster of bleary-eyed individuals he has just questioned.

Lenny turns a corner. His Death-shaped shadow follows.

She watches him closely, noting the way he stops abruptly and tilts his head. It looks as though he is listening for something. So when he sets off once more, rather decisively this time, Mara is fascinated to find their lost Tele precisely where Lenny evidently determined.

Yes, very intriguing, this Hyper.

Blair has her back pressed against a sooty wall until her Imperial declares, 'So, hating sticky buns was just a means of distraction, right?'

'Plagues!' What a funny curse Blair blurts at his sudden appearance. Death wonders if she should take it personally. Then, impressively, the Tele is furious a moment later. 'How the hell did you find me?'

Death has been wondering this herself. She's not even entirely sure how Lenny knew his assignment was no longer in the castle. But Mara frets not – she will find out soon enough.

'I need to know that your dislike for sticky buns was only a tactic used to get rid of me,' Lenny responds evenly, folding his arms.

What is it with these sticky buns? They certainly weren't around in Death's time, but she is starting to feel a bit left out.

'Well, it wasn't,' Blair bites. 'In fact, my disdain for them is only outshined by my loathing for you.'

Moonlight carves out the unimpressed look on the Imperial's face. 'That's a bit dramatic. Even for you.'

'Leave, gingersnap,' Blair demands. 'Before I change my mind about letting you.'

Lenny promptly ignores her threat. 'How did you escape?'

A mocking laugh. 'It doesn't matter. You should be *thanking* me. Now you can go back to your sad, little life as an Imperial and stop pretending like you're guarding me.'

Mara leans against the wall, making herself comfortable. The show is about to begin.

Lenny pulls that mask from his face to display the confusion beneath. 'I'm not following.'

'A shocker to no one.'

He carries on, undeterred. 'Where the hell do you think you're going?'

'Anywhere but Ilya,' Blair retorts sharply.

Oh, this is better than Death could have hoped.

Lenny shakes his head. 'Let me get this straight.' He makes an admirable show of glancing around the shadowed slums. 'You want to run away from your cushy life? To live on the streets?'

'No, I want to live in Tando,' she blurts. Blair can't seem to stifle the onslaught of slippery words. 'I am getting out of here. And I don't care if I have to cross the Scorches to do it.'

Death cannot imagine this well-manicured girl surviving such brutality. She has already gathered far fiercer souls from the sandy grave, each of them fools scrambling towards a better life. But Fate laughs in the face of hope.

'The Scorches?' The Imperial practically laughs. 'Paedyn barely survived crossing it—'

'Oh, yes,' the Tele mocks. 'Because the Ordinary is just the pinnacle of strength.'

'Blair, just listen to me for a second!'

Mara blinks. It seems that gingersnap has . . . well, snapped.

He sighs, deeply. 'Let's just talk about this, okay? Why do you want to leave Ilya? Aside from a single day trapped in your room, the life you live is pretty damn good.'

Blair flicks a strand of lilac hair behind her shoulder. 'Of course you would think that.'

'I grew up here.' The Imperial gestures to the crumbling city, his expression uncharacteristically stern. 'In these slums. So, yeah. I would say your life is pretty damn good.'

Blair considers this. Her look of disdain never falters. 'Fine. You don't need to know my reasonings. I just want out of here.' That brown gaze darkens further still. 'And you're in my way.'

Death wonders what it is she wishes to run from. Surely something tragically human, like a public embarrassment or a blemish that simply won't fade. But that satirical thought passes quickly, as it does not feel right for this soul.

Mara, as vigilant as ever, is beginning to believe that there is more to Miss Archer than meets the eye. Perhaps her stony exterior is the product of being hurt one too many times before. Death can sympathize with harsh women – life forced them to become so.

'I can't just let you run away,' Lenny manages through an exasperated laugh. 'The king would be furious with me. Not to mention your father—'

'He will understand better than most,' Blair muses.

Pinching the bridge of his nose in a dramatic show of

annoyance, the Imperial mutters, 'It doesn't matter. I could lose my position as an Imperial if I just let you waltz from the castle.'

A good point, Mara thinks.

'Firstly—' the Tele raises a finger in Lenny's face '—let's not pretend that you're aiding me in any way. Secondly—' another finger '—you are a Hyper. A buffer between Paedyn and me. Everyone knows you're not capable of handling *me*.'

This doesn't seem to sit well with the Imperial. Once again, his strength and capability have been called into question. 'The king expects me to keep you in the castle,' he says between a flash of teeth.

'So find another job.'

The moon dances off the Imperial's cerise curls when he shakes his head in disbelief. 'You really don't get it, do you? Some of us are forced to actually work for what we have.' He inches closer to the Tele. 'I wasn't handed a cushy life or some ridiculously powerful ability. I got here on my own.'

Lenny makes sense to Death. He is honest, determined to make something of himself. This is the type of human Mara prefers – one who does not hide behind embellishments. This Imperial is boldly bare.

'Here?' Blair scoffs. 'Your big dream was to be a lazy guard?'

'Yes, because I want to be respected despite my ability,' Lenny counters with that admirable candor. 'I know being an Imperial means nothing to you, but it is everything to me.'

Vulnerability seeps into each word, and that alone takes strength. 'And if you run away, it will only prove what everyone already thinks of me – that I'm just another weak Hyper.'

Mara tilts her head at him. It's a bit ironic, really, that he doesn't seem to realize how much strength vulnerability like this requires.

Lenny draws a deep breath. Blair remains unflinching.

Several seconds pass. Death leans in.

'You can't stop me, gingersnap.'

The Imperial clasps his hands together. 'Fine. Then we are doing this my way.'

Blair finds this comical. 'Excuse me?'

'You can't just take off,' Lenny explains. 'You'll ruin everything I've built for myself. Not to mention that someone – whether that be your parents or the king – will always be searching for you.' His next words incite a flicker of doubt from the Tele. 'You'll never truly be free from whatever it is you so desperately wish to escape.'

Blair says nothing. Her lack of snide remark only spurs on the Imperial. 'We have to find a better way to make you disappear. Ensure you can live your life as you please without fear of being found.' He pauses to throw her a skeptical look. 'Assuming that is what you want.'

'It is.'

Death thinks the Tele's answer seems a bit too eager.

As if noticing that herself, Blair adds a lazy scoff. 'And you are going to come up with this plan?'

Lenny runs a hand through his unruly hair. Mara, eternally opinionated, concludes that it needs to be trimmed. 'If it means I don't lose everything I've worked so hard for, then yes, I'll come up with a damn good plan.'

'I doubt that,' Blair mocks. 'But I'll give you a week. When you inevitably fail, I'm disappearing.'

She brushes past him. He trails her at a respectable distance. Still, they somehow manage to argue all the way to the castle.

The Tele uses her mind to repeatedly pelt the Hyper with pebbles while Death watches from afar, lurking in the shadows like the living so dare to assume.

How incredibly hopeless, these two beings.

And yet, defiantly, their souls still strain to meet.

Mara thinks on such absurdity as she strolls through the quiet castle. Leaving the perplexing pair to squabble all the way to their room, Death proceeds to haunt the shadowed halls in peace. It's quite late, ensuring every servant has found a pillow to rest their head upon. Still, the inky corridors echo with the sound of dozing Imperials, their snoring thoroughly rattling the windowpanes.

Death isn't quite sure what it is she searches for. Something exciting would be most appreciated. Though Mara hardly looks it from the outside (she is not one for expressions, remember), she finds great joy in the unexpected. Though, there is little that still surprises her.

As if summoned by such a challenge, the king rounds a dark corner.

Hmm.

It seems Death stands corrected. Stumbling upon Kitt Azer at this hour is certainly worth her bewilderment.

'Mara,' he says, sounding equally perplexed and pleased by her presence.

It's still odd, being acknowledged by the living – or rather, the doomed.

Death might have forgotten her own name if the king had asked for it a moment later. Such intimacy has grown foreign to her. No soul – this side of the eternity she serves – has ever cared to call her anything but an atrocity. A monster.

Mara's gaze trails over this king. He does not look like the many others she has dragged to the Mors – harsh and weathered. No, moonlight drapes over the soft features of a boy forced to become so much more. Blond hair waves atop his head, unruly with the remnants of sleep, though his green gaze is alert. Every feature is oddly strong yet subtle, unique yet fitting.

Death must admit, with a practiced flippancy, that this man is hardly terrible to look at. In fact, she beheld a variant of this face many times before. The shadow of familiarity there, the memory of another who shared his countenance, is precisely what drew her back to Ilya at all.

'Why are you awake at this hour?' Mara asks evenly. Her

voice has gotten very little use in the last several decades, so the soft sound of it occasionally startles her. Even she agrees that it hardly fits with Death's description.

Kitt smiles. The action suits him. 'I could ask you the same thing.'

Death answers truthfully – another thing the living would likely find surprising. 'I don't sleep.'

The king runs a hand through his tangled, golden hair. 'Yes, it does feel that way, doesn't it? I can't remember the last time I slept through the night either.'

Not quite what Mara meant, but she enjoys watching humans draw their own conclusions. Just as Kitt had done this morning when deeming her a Healer. She considers this a compliment, actually. A lifetime ago, she yearned to be addressed as such.

Death eyes this man who stands with one foot in the grave. 'What does a king do when he cannot sleep?'

'Wander,' he sighs. 'Think.'

'A better use of one's time than unconsciousness.'

With a soft chuckle, Kitt leans against the wall to look out a moon-drenched window. 'Your fellow Healers certainly don't agree.'

'Well, they don't wish to spend any more time with themselves than they have to.' Mara laces her fingers. 'So they beg for sleep.'

Kitt stares at Death. She thinks, biasedly, that he looks rather awed by her. 'Is that why you are awake? To spend more time with yourself?'

Mara's stoic expression remains. 'In a sense. I am searching the shadows for myself.'

The moon leans in, peering through the panes of glass.

'Do you not know who you are, Mara?'

Death likes the sound of her name. She had forgotten.

'Not anymore,' she answers simply.

Kitt wears the look of one who has been utterly seen for the first time. 'And . . . and you plan to figure that out in the middle of the night?'

'Is it not the darkest parts of ourselves that ultimately make us who we are?'

The king can't help but smile. 'Perhaps you are a Scholar.'

A long moment passes. Maybe a dozen. Death no longer has a heartbeat to count.

Dipping her head, Mara steps from the puddle of moonlight. She has never been good at farewells. So she flees them altogether.

Nearly halfway down the hall, Kitt's voice has her halting. 'Mara?'

Yes, she quite likes hearing her name. And it has nothing to do with the young king saying it, of course.

Death turns to face his fading soul – a flickering, muted blue.

'May I join you in your search?' he asks with a touch of humor.

Mara tilts her head at him. 'You are looking for yourself?'

Kitt's long strides carry him swiftly towards Death.

Fitting, this depiction of his fate.

'No,' the king admits. 'I'm hoping to find something far better.'

CHAPTER 6

An explosion rattles the coach.
 I'm thrown against the seat, my ears ringing.

Time slows; vision blurs.

Shouting Imperials crowd around me while the slums erupt beyond their cocoon.

Stone crumbles from buildings, spitting debris on those scrambling in the streets.

My chest heaves with every piercing scream that wafts from the smoke.

I shut my stinging eyes.

This is all my doing.

Another bomb has the coach shuddering.

How did we get here?

Just a handful of hours ago, I was safely in my study.

The morning was quiet. I spent most of it staring down at my ink-stained hand.

There was no ring on my finger, but I felt the weight of my engagement nonetheless. Paedyn was still so stubbornly the same girl I once knew, despite the killer she became. It had been mere days since she so selflessly accepted my proposal. The hope this former Silver Savior clung to was just as naive and as annoyingly admirable as ever. But her moral compass guided me to say precisely what she needed to hear – promise of a united Ilya.

Now she wore that ring like a shackle, bound to the duty she felt for this kingdom.

'Your Majesty?'

A Healer was inspecting me, just like every morning.

'Hmm?' I looked up at him distantly.

Eli's smile was tight. 'I asked if His Majesty could please turn his head to the side.'

'Of course,' I murmured before obliging.

My gaze frequently fell to a flyer atop my desk, the same one that was distributed throughout the city. It detailed the story I spun to coax Paedyn into accepting my proposal. Uniting the Elites and Ordinaries so the surrounding cities resumed trade was hardly motivated by resources – though Ilya truly ran low. No, it was trusting kingdoms and open borders I craved.

Eli's frigid fingers slid from my throat. 'That is all for today, my young King.'

I tipped my head in thanks as the probing Healers and whispering Scholars slipped out of the study. A shock of disappointment coursed through me when none of the passing faces belonged to Mara. This was alarming. I was engaged when meeting the intriguing woman, and that unfortunate fact still remained.

My betrothal to Paedyn Gray was the price I must pay for greatness.

Ironic, that an Ordinary would spark the spread of Elites.

A booming explosion startles me back to the present.

I blink against the haze of smoke, my eyes watering.

Kai no longer sits across from me in this coach open to the sky, pretending as though he doesn't see Paedyn's knee resting against my own. Our interrupted parade was more an excuse to spend time with him than it was to celebrate my complicated engagement. And for a short time, amid that peaceful promenade through the kingdom, I nearly forgot Paedyn's presence.

That is, until she begged to extend the festivities to her home. Just as I knew she would.

Admirably predictable.

'Stay down, Your Majesty!'

I duck at the Imperial's barked order, hating that I'm the only one cowering in this coach. Kai is off being the Enforcer while my bride-to-be is blatantly defying orders. She disappeared into the chaos after slipping through the wall of Imperials, leaving me here to sit in the discomfort of my decision. Alone. Forgotten.

This destruction is my doing.

Like a morbid symphony, screams crescendo all around.

I am not a monster.

This had to be done – Calum agreed. That seems important to remind myself, perhaps because this guilt is not mine alone to bear. But I needed disarray, a tangible defiance. The kingdom has boldly murmured their objection to an Ordinary queen – I only raised their voices.

The Trials must commence. And this will force my betrothed into them. Force her to unknowingly do my bidding.

Smoke fills my lungs until I'm choking on the consequences of my actions.

I am not a monster.

The ringing in my ears brings no reprieve from the sound of panicked horses and wailing Elites. I can see nothing from where I crouch on the floor of this coach, coddled by a swarm of Imperials. The heavy crown on my head is slipping, and I'm certain I look the part of a helpless royal. I suppose that is what I am, really. A king still overshadowed by the weak brother he used to be.

But not for much longer.

I tear the crown off, letting it clang onto the floor beside me.

This is my mess – I should at least be in the middle of it.

I stand to my feet despite the Imperials' protests. The ruin I ordered sprawls before me, all crumbling stone and scrambling bodies. Ribbons of flame feast on tattered banners, devouring the carts of several merchants. The street is shrouded in a thick smoke that blurs the chaos within.

But it's the scattered bodies that hold my horrified gaze.

Blood coats the cobblestones. It's an obvious consequence that hadn't occurred to me.

People were going to die before my plan even began.

That soft part of me, the weakness Father despised, shies away at the realization of what it is I've done. In fact, I'm tempted to forfeit the fate I've meticulously crafted for myself if it means saving those in the path of my plotted destiny. And that only confirms what I already know to be true.

Kitt Azer needs to die.

A tender heart has no place in history. It must cease beating if I wish to be great.

So when a bomb erupts mere feet from me, I fear some greater power may have misunderstood my metaphor.

The coach trembles, and I'm thrown to the floor with the impact. My skull meets something hard on the way down. I might have yelled; I'm not sure. The world has gone quiet.

I look up at the smoky sky above. Imperials lean over the coach's sides, nudging their way into my line of sight. Their mouths move beneath the white masks they wear. There is a dull humming in my ears. I haven't the slightest clue what they are saying. In fact, I feel quite cold.

My gaze drifts to the bench beside me. It is where Kai had reminisced with me during our journey from the castle. It was like we were brothers again. And I would very much like to cling to that moment.

Though, it seems the seat has already been taken.

Another figure now occupies the plush bench, legs crossed comfortably. She is slender beneath the dark cloak slung over her shoulders. Auburn hair slips just past her collarbones when she tilts her head at me. And though her eyes are what some might describe as a common brown, I doubt I've seen a pair so piercing.

Mara.

She stares down at me, paying no heed to the commotion beyond. Rather, she wears that look of veiled intrigue. It's as though she is waiting for something.

I open my mouth – to say what, I'm not sure – when the world suddenly comes rushing back. An Imperial pulls me onto the bench opposite Mara, informing me of our immediate departure. Every muffled word grows in volume until the sound of mayhem is a dull roar in my ears.

I'm about to demand my brother be brought to me when his form emerges from the smoke. And while I shouldn't be surprised to see Paedyn held in his arms, it still manages to sting.

Of course he ensured she was okay before returning to me.

I shrug off the jealousy that taps me on the shoulder, begging for a reaction. Instead, I stiffly await their return to the coach. When an Imperial throws open the door, ushering my Enforcer and betrothed inside, I glance over at the Healer occupying their seat.

Except, she no longer does. Mara is gone.

I blink at the empty bench before Kai and Paedyn are sliding onto it. The coach begins moving before they have even settled across from me, both bloody and panting. Tears brim in Paedyn's gaze when it falls on the scarlet-stained hem of her dress. 'What happened?' she gasps, voice breaking.

Kai scans the chaos blurring past. 'We can't talk now. There are ears everywhere.' The coach rattles across uneven cobblestones, swerving between scattered stone. My brother's scrutiny slides to me. 'Are you all right? I ensured you were surrounded by Imperials.'

I swallow. 'I am fine.'

I am a monster.

'Who would do this?' Paedyn whispers.

A monster.

'A monster.'

My gaze snaps to Kai when he utters the words my mind screams.

No. No, he is not supposed to think that about me. Not him. This is *for* him. For us. He will see that soon – he *has* to see that.

My brother's gaze falls on Paedyn. It always does. 'This is a message.'

I look away. The smoking street slips past.

This was a message. One I have scrawled across my life. In the Plague I swallowed, the betrothal to a woman my brother wants, the pain I must cause before gifting power – there is nothing I won't do for those I love.

And I only know how to love Kai.

I am a monster. I am a king.

Perhaps one cannot exist without the other.

CHAPTER 7

Death wonders how long Blair Archer can pretend to read her book.

After five days of imprisonment within her own room, the Tele remains on the same page. Mara, selfishly, finds this rather vexing, as she would very much like to continue reading over her shoulder. Although, such feigned engrossment is rather clever on Blair's part, as it helps to curb gingersnap's (the Tele's nickname, of course) appetite for constant commentary.

Rather than standing outside the door, Lenny has taken a liking to joining the Tele in her boredom – and subsequently, Mara's. Their relentless quarreling has thoroughly entertained Death over the past few days, complete with the mental throwing of objects and several detailed threats. Lenny manages to complain about his stiff neck nearly every hour (he sleeps on a patch of floor with the occasional gifted blanket), while Blair stares glassily at that book, blissfully ignoring him.

They have yet to tear each other apart, but Death is holding out hope.

It is a good thing Mara still enjoys their company – though draining at times – because she has no other souls to stalk at present. After the parade bombing, Death thought it best to adamantly avoid the king until she was prepared to answer what questions he will undoubtedly have. You see, she hadn't planned to appear under such circumstances, but Kitt's immediate danger in that moment had drawn Mara to him. Their connection is one she has never experienced, for Death feels his fading soul as if it were her own. This human's demise is unique – but he need not know that.

You see, Death clutches the truth closely, as it is the only thing one is allowed to bring with them into the afterlife.

Blair drops the book onto her bed, sighing in relief when Lenny slips from her room for the second time this evening (he drinks a lot of water, and the Tele has banned him from using her washroom). So, Death settles onto the comforter beside her and watches the sun slowly sink beyond the line of windows. She finds this rather peaceful, but Blair's scowl at the sight seems to indicate otherwise.

Ahh. Mara understands (unlike the rumors, she is not entirely void of empathy). Life is slowly slipping by – without the Tele.

She seems to blame herself for this, as though such a punishment is deserved. Mara often wonders about this young woman — who she is and what she wishes to become. Blair Archer is a mystery that Death intends to solve.

The Tele throws a pillow over her head. If Mara were to guess — she often does when it comes to humans — it seems to her like Blair is attempting to smother a memory. This theory is only confirmed when the Tele sits up suddenly, gasping for air.

Death blinks at the outburst. Then at the look of defiance Blair summons to her features.

The bizarre woman clasps her hands together. Swallows thickly.

Mara watches her pick mindlessly at the skin on her left palm. It is a habit she's observed before.

Yes, what is it that haunts a woman of such formidability?

The distant sound of someone approaching draws the attention of both Blair and the shadow of Death beside her.

Click. Click. Click.

The Tele rolls her eyes, fervently.

She seems to know this approaching person.

The realization summons a short woman with unnaturally stern expressions. She throws open the door (she, too, must have a key) and clicks towards Blair in a pair of tall heels. 'Unacceptable.' Cropped brown hair swishes with the declaration. 'Absolutely unacceptable.'

Mara flicks her gaze between the women. Their scowls alone bear enough resemblance to deem them related.

This must be the Tele Tyrant's mother (again, not Death's nickname).

Blair swipes up the book to continue her charade of reading. 'This should be good,' she mocks.

Hmm.

Not particularly close with her mother, Death gathers.

'It has been five days, Blair.'

Based on the Tele's hardening expression, it seems the use of her name is hardly a good thing.

'Five days that should have been spent training and apprenticing with your father,' the woman seethes. Her heels click against the floor until she is looming over the bed. 'But no. You are trapped in this room because even the king thinks you can't handle an Ordinary.' She meets her daughter's gaze before landing the final blow. 'And he is right.'

To Blair's credit, she keeps her head high and her mouth shut.

It seems the woman despises a lack of reaction, so she happily spits more malice into the silence. 'I didn't raise you to be weak.'

'Really?' Blair finally snaps. 'Because weakness runs in your blood, not mine.'

It happens so quickly, the slap across Blair's face. Even Death is startled by this mother's willingness to strike her own daughter, though not entirely surprised. It is those closest to us who are often most cruel. Mara knows this firsthand, for she, too, had been wronged. But Death was quick to remedy that grave error.

The force of that strike has the Tele's head whipping to the side. And yet, she still manages to emanate that typical smugness. For it was she who struck the harder blow.

The woman breathes heavily beside Mara while her daughter's cheek grows red and splotchy. Blair stares up at her mother, decidedly unafraid. It is a look that has likely been well practiced over the years.

'I won't let your inadequacy ruin this family,' the woman declares. 'You will continue our legacy.'

Blair forces a biting smile. 'I'll disgrace us all.'

'Then you will have proved me right.' The woman's tone is smug. Death sees where Blair gets it from. 'And I know how much you hate that.'

They glare at each other, displaying the harshness they share. A long moment passes in which they revel in their joint animosity. Then the Tele's mother clicks her heels towards the open door. 'Oh, and that Ordinary is engaged to the king,' she says over a shoulder. 'If she becomes queen, you will answer to her. And she will never set you free.'

Engaged.

This is news to Death.

Blair blows out a shaky breath when her mother finally

strides from the room. She then lifts a hand to her stinging cheek, anger flooding her features.

'Well, she seems lovely.'

The Imperial's sarcasm only has Blair rolling her watering eyes. He steps hesitantly into the room, his brow creasing beneath that white mask.

'Does she always speak to you that way?'

Now his tone is genuine.

This human is kind, Mara observes, not for the first time. His soul is warm, inviting – the type that will be mourned. This thought has something within her, long dead and cold, twinging with jealousy.

With a deep breath, the Tele wipes all emotion from her features – straightens her spine, lifts her chin. 'Why don't you just eavesdrop on our next conversation to see how it compares?'

'No, I wouldn't do that.' Lenny sounds offended. 'I only heard because the door was open, but I wouldn't go out of my way to invade the little privacy you now have.'

'So,' Blair starts, disinterested, 'you have super hearing but don't use it to eavesdrop?'

Mara is beginning to better understand this Hyper ability of his (such possession of power is used loosely, remember).

The Imperial folds his arms over the rumpled uniform he slept in. Death has begun to realize that he owns little else. 'Not if I don't want to. It's . . . it's like a dial,' he explains distantly. 'I can turn my senses up or down whenever I want.'

This still does not explain how he recognized Mara's presence – yet another mystery for her to decipher.

Blair's gaze flicks back to the book she is still pretending to read. 'How disappointing.'

'Yeah, we get it,' Lenny sighs out in defeat. 'I have a shitty power.'

'Well, yes.' The Tele doesn't bother looking at him. 'But it's even more disappointing that you aren't using said shitty power to your advantage.'

The Imperial simply stares at her. 'Oh.'

'I have fun with my ability all the time.' The words have hardly left her lips before that purple ball Lenny so loves to bounce is hitting him in the face once again. 'See?'

This object is frequently materializing to cause bodily harm, Death observes quietly.

'I know what you're doing,' the Imperial declares while rubbing his forehead. 'You're deflecting. Why won't you talk about your mom?'

'Because she's a bitch,' Blair answers simply.

Lenny snorts. 'Must run in the family.'

'No.' The Tele snaps her book shut. 'We are made this way.'

The Imperial voices Death's confusion. 'Are you referring to, uh, bitches in general? Or . . . ?'

'If you're so concerned about *my* relationship with *my* mother,' Blair bites, 'help me escape it. Our deal is almost up.'

'About that.' Lenny sits on the edge of the bed, ignoring the abhorrent look on the Tele's face. Mara sits beside him, and to her veiled disappointment, no one objects. 'I ran into Paedyn on her way to dinner with the king. And . . .' He chuckles darkly. 'She still very much hates you.'

'Obviously,' Blair snaps. 'You tell me that instead of mentioning they are engaged? With how much you talk, I at least figured the important stuff would slip out.'

Lenny smiles timidly. 'Right. Sorry about that. I forget you don't have a shitty ability that allows you to overhear conversations.' His words tumble out in a rush. 'See, the day we started this unfortunate assignment, Pae came and visited me outside your door. I figured you heard the commotion she caused trying to get to you, and our conversation about the engagement.'

'Well, I didn't.' The Tele swallows her snarl. 'What the hell is Kitt doing marrying that Ordinary?'

'The right thing,' Lenny supplies. 'Despite Ilya needing resources, uniting the Elites and Ordinaries is the right thing to do. And Paedyn can help do that.'

'Of course you would feel that way.' There is a sharp edge to her voice. 'You are practically an Ordinary yourself.'

'Fine,' the Imperial admits. 'I may be next to Ordinary, but you're the one who is trapped in this room, powerless.'

A fine point, Mara thinks. She finds herself continually rooting for this young man. Even Death has deemed him quite enjoyable.

'Powerless?' Blair scoffs.

She is, regrettably, a bit harder to enjoy.

Smugly, she adds, 'I can walk out that door whenever I like.'

'So why didn't you?' Lenny throws his hands up in exasperation. 'No one was stopping you from running away until a few days ago. You had your whole life to leave. But you didn't.'

Mara flicks her gaze between them. The Imperial's expression remains earnest, imploring. But the Tele wears a mask much colder, cutting. It is as though she wavers on the edge of something egregiously irreversible. Like a terrible truth sits on the tip of her tongue.

Finally, she settles on a deflecting demand. 'What is the plan?'

The shadow of sadness that darkens Lenny's face does not go unnoticed by Death. He wishes to understand this temperamental Tele, bridge the cavern between them. But Blair refuses to meet him halfway.

Humans are such difficult creatures, Mara has come to remember. They have a nasty habit of making everything exceedingly harder for themselves.

'Fine,' Lenny sighs. 'But you're not going to like it.'

'That's hardly surprising.'

The Imperial paces a crooked path across the floor. 'Okay, well, as I mentioned, Paedyn wants you dead. You want to flee Ilya without anyone looking for you. And I want to still have some dignity left by the time we're done with this.'

'If you had any to begin with,' Blair sneers beneath her breath.

'You know what?' Lenny shakes his head. 'You are almost funny, Blair Archer. If only you used your powers for good.'

She almost smiles at that. Death nearly does as well.

The moment is fleeting. 'So?' The Tele huffs. 'Get on with the plan, gingersnap.'

'All right, all right.'

He looks slightly concerned for his safety.

Blair seems to relish the sight.

Death is thoroughly enjoying herself.

'So . . . Paedyn kind of needs to kill you.'

CHAPTER 8
Ritt

A splotch of ink mars my white sleeve.

Sighing, I dab at it with a handkerchief. This only smears the stain more thoroughly, forcing me to shrug on my suit coat and smother it. I then loosen the tie around my throat before returning to the task at hand.

A blank piece of parchment sits atop the cluttered desk, awaiting the spillage of my thoughts. I had already filled the one prior with a recent and complicated discovery. Because that is how I manage my muddled mind – hastily and with a flurry of scribbled letters. And yet, the nib of my pen hovers over this pristine page.

I cannot seem to find the right words to describe her. Perhaps there aren't any.

Clearing my throat, I figure it's best to start at the beginning.

My pen meets the page.

I met a woman named Mara. She was in my study bu

I pull back suddenly, blinking at the freshly carved words now fading before my very eyes.

Awed, I watch each letter shy away from the page. They disappear slowly, as though the parchment is greedily swallowing each trail of ink. Then, as if I'd never written a word, the page returns to its spotless state.

Several seconds pass before I remember to take a breath.

'What the hell happened?' I mutter, half expecting the magical paper to respond.

Hesitantly, I try out another string of words.

Mara was in my coach during the parade bombing. I don't know how or

The ink vanishes.

I lean back in my chair, utterly bewildered.

There is some reasonable explanation for this. There has to be.

I shuffle through my piles of parchment, scattering scribbled notes in every direction. On the corner of a crumpled document, I scrawl:

Who is Mara?

The words drift away.

Hastily, I pull another page from the stack. This time, I only bother etching her name – then I watch the four letters disappear.

I'm suddenly scribbling those four letters on every surface – madly, incessantly.

Mara. Mara. MARA.

Nothing. Nothing. Nothing.

It is as though she doesn't exist. As though the letters rebel against the very idea of her.

I run a hand down my face. Perhaps I really am going mad like everyone so readily believed at the beginning of my reign.

I stare at the first page that rejected Mara's name. Then, tentatively, I press my pen to the picky parchment once again.

Kitt.

Nothing. Nothing happens, and that means something.

The word remains.

I stare down at my name. It looks entirely unremarkable.

I try a sentence next.

I am in my study.

When the words don't disappear, I suddenly become aware of how ridiculous this all is. I'm glaring at curls of ink, as though they are about to jump off the page.

I'm just seeing things.

To prove my own insanity, I lazily scrawl one final sentence.

I'm going to figure out who Mara is.

All evidence of my message slips away. And though I'm not entirely sure I am of sound mind, there is no denying the blank page before me. I might have called a witness into the room if my lungs hadn't tightened to the point of pain. The foreign feeling startles me, enough so to have a cough rattling in my chest.

That is when the chill skitters down my spine.

I have felt it before. It's a sort of tugging at my soul, a presence of something infinitely *more*.

I look up from the page where her name refused to remain. And there Mara stands.

Her auburn hair falls effortlessly atop the dark cloak blanketing her figure. As stoic as ever, she drags her piercing gaze over me. 'Sharing your thoughts with paper again?'

'Trying to,' I say slowly, my skepticism evident. 'What are you doing here?'

'Seeing if you're well.'

'You're a thorough Healer.'

I hold her unwavering stare.

'Hmm.' There is that intrigued hum of hers. 'Are you going somewhere?'

When her eyes flick over me, I'm suddenly reminded that I have somewhere to be. 'Oh, yes. There is a gathering while we wait to see if Paedyn completes the first of her Trials.'

'Trials.' She says the word like it's the punchline of a joke I missed. 'Elites do love displaying the power of Death.'

Confusion creases my brow. 'The Purging Trials aren't meant to kill the contestants.'

'Hmm.' She seems to find this interesting as well. 'What about these Trials? Are they meant to rid you of your betrothed?'

'Not yet. She is useful to me.' I'm unable to stop the words before they come careening out of my mouth. 'Wow—'

I nearly laugh in shock at the despicable truth '—you must think I'm a horrible person.'

'No.' Mara eyes me closely. 'You are much more complicated than that.'

I clear my throat when that clenching feeling returns to my lungs.

And with every cough, that eerie presence, that beckoning of my very soul, grows.

I lift my gaze to the watchful woman. And something cowers within me.

'Who are you?'

My murmured words don't seem to surprise her. I doubt little would. 'We have already met.'

'You were in that coach when the bomb erupted,' I blurt. 'I know you were.' Every bit of my stifled confusion comes spilling out. 'Now you're here, and I get this tightening in my chest.'

My skepticism is met with silence.

'I can feel you.' My tone grows urgent. 'Like a . . . like a pair of eyes on me from across a room or a cool breeze on the back of my neck. So tell me who you really are, Mara.' I stand slowly from my seat with palms braced against the desk. 'Because you're not a Healer.'

'No,' she agrees simply. 'I'm not. You are the one who determined I was.'

I shake my head in frustration and feel the crown atop it

begin to slip. 'I don't understand – just help me understand. How are you always there when I am . . .'

'Dying?'

My mouth parts as I stare at her. If the pensive look on her face ever budged, I might have thought she was joking. 'Dying? No, I'm not—'

'You were six feet from Death at that parade,' she cuts in evenly. 'Six.'

My chest heaves. 'Why were you there? I saw you on that bench. And then you just . . . vanished.'

She tilts her head at me, as though she pities my ignorance. 'Six feet is close enough to warrant my presence. And every time you cough, the Plague is inching you closer to me.'

Exasperation makes me desperate. 'Who the hell are you?'

Her dark eyes bore into mine. 'You're asking the wrong question.'

My blood chills; lungs tighten; soul slips.

'Why can't I write about you?' I fight to keep my voice even. 'Your name . . . It just disappears.'

'I cannot be contained.' She says this as though it should be obvious. 'Not by language or time.'

'*What* the hell are you?' I breathe.

'I thought you wanted to see me.' Her face is unreadable. 'Why else would you take the Plague?'

'For power,' I say sternly.

'Or to die knowing you tried everything to get it.'

It feels as though the room is spinning around me. 'You thought I took the Plague to see you.' My voice is hoarse. 'That would mean . . .'

I watch a soft smile pull at her lips for the first time.

'Now, a foot and a half separates you from Death.'

I blink at the beautiful woman before me. She stands on the other side of my desk – a foot and a half away.

I attempt a weak laugh. 'That's absurd.'

'You live in a kingdom that was magically blessed with powers from a Plague, and you don't even bother to ask why,' she reminds plainly. 'Death should hardly be shocking.'

'It's not Death I'm unfamiliar with,' I stammer. 'It's . . .' I gesture to the length of her. 'It's *you*.'

Her brows lift, ever so slightly. 'Surely you've seen a woman before.'

I pinch the bridge of my nose, just as Father used to. 'Yes, I've seen a woman before. Just never one that claimed to be Death.'

Mara considers this for a long moment. 'I retrieved your father's soul from outside the arena. He had a stab wound to his chest and throat. His soul was rather stubborn.'

She stares at me intently, as though her words haven't just paralyzed me. 'Why . . .' I swallow. 'Why are you telling me this?'

'I don't get to have many conversations with the living. Or the mostly living,' she amends.

I can do little else but gawk at her. This is insanity, and yet, I indulge it.

If this is truly Death, I don't wish to have her as an enemy.

'You're not afraid of me,' Mara observes.

A knock at the door nearly makes me jump.

'Your Majesty, it's time for your entrance,' an Imperial calls from the hallway.

My chest heaves. 'In a moment!'

I turn my attention back to Mara, Death, *something*.

She offers the most subdued of smiles.

No, this cannot be the same Death that strikes fear into every beating heart.

'Go live,' she urges softly. 'While you still can.'

And just like her name on a page, she vanishes without a trace.

CHAPTER 9
Mara

*T*hump. Thump. Thump.

The ball Lenny consistently bounces against the wall has deflated slightly. Even it has grown tired of his games.

Occasionally, the Imperial stops to stare longingly out the row of windows. Above, the moon glares back, glowing brightly against the blackened sky. That streaming, pale light pools in the concern carved on Lenny's freckled brow. And for the better part of an hour, Death has occupied herself by watching that worry only deepen.

This is hardly the most interesting part of her day – no, that would have been when she entered the king's study as Mara and left as Death. And she is not entirely sure what to do with that. No soul has ever met Death and lived to tell the tale.

Perhaps, then, Mara should take advantage of this rarity.

Blair turns a page of her book (shockingly) from where she lounges in bed. 'You are suspiciously quiet.'

'Well . . .' Lenny doesn't turn to face her flaunting of comfort and instead continues to sit stiffly on the floor, leaning against her bedpost. 'Since you want to crush my windpipe every time I speak, I figured it was safer if I didn't.'

'Maybe you aren't as dumb as you look,' she says, rather sincerely.

The Imperial shakes his head and returns to his boredom.

Thump. Thump. Thump.

Blair clears her throat. 'Have the festivities started?'

Mara gets the sense that this Tele is unsure what to do with a melancholy Lenny. He appeases her with a dull 'Yup. They are happily drinking and gossiping.'

The party is taking place on the other side of the castle.

This Hyper ability is fascinating, Death admits.

'She's going to be fine,' Blair huffs reluctantly.

Slowly, Lenny turns to peer at his assignment over the bed. That is when those brown eyes drag over Death yet again.

If she had a heartbeat, it might have stumbled.

'Wow.' The Hyper rests his chin on the quilt, looking up at Blair. He is completely oblivious to the spiral he's sent Mara into. 'Are you complimenting Paedyn's strength and skill to survive this Trial?'

The Tele scowls at him. 'No. I'm simply stating that somehow, she always ends up getting what she wants.'

'Come on, Blair.' Lenny returns a dull look. 'Her father died. She was forced to survive on the streets.'

'Exactly,' she says a bit quickly. 'She was free. She got to do whatever she pleased. And then one day, she made it into the same Purging Trials that some of us have prepared for our whole lives. But not just that.' She laughs, and the sound is bitter. 'No, she managed to get away with the fact that she is an Ordinary. Excelled in the Trials. Toyed with both princes. Then she was discovered as a traitor, killed the king, and fled.'

The words gush out of her, as though a dam has broken free behind her tongue. 'And just like everyone else,' Blair continues with a humorless laugh, 'I thought she wouldn't get away with it. But here we are. Paedyn Gray is now engaged to a king.'

Yes, Death really must meet this woman.

'Is that why you've always hated her?' Lenny murmurs carefully.

Blair sighs. 'I envy her, okay? She is free.' The words are hollow. 'Besides, she is precisely who my mother wishes I was – without the Ordinary bit, obviously.'

'That is . . .' The Imperial shakes his head at her. 'Very human of you.'

Lenny then steals a moment to simply look at the woman before him. Mara watches him take in the simple blouse she wears, the fitted pants beneath, and the intimidating expression above. Death can see it on his face — the slow realization that there might be a softness smothered beneath.

Suddenly aware of her sincerity, Blair morphs back into that unfeeling shell of herself. 'Shut up, gingersnap.'

'Such kindness you exude,' Lenny says warmly. Reverting back to their usual bickering, he leans over the bed to tap the spine of her book. 'Hey, what is it that you're always reading?'

Death would like to know as well. It seems she will have to find her own copy to discover what awaits on the next page.

'None of your business,' Blair snaps.

'Interesting title.'

'That's it.' She snaps the book shut — dramatic, since she wasn't actually trying to read it. 'I'm leaving.'

Lenny watches her stand from the bed's warm embrace. 'Where do you think you're going?'

'Loot,' she informs. 'I'm sick of this room. And you.'

Death follows curiously, leaning over Blair's shoulder when she stops before the fireplace. It's rather unassuming, this stone hearth, though it lies empty and cold. The Tele fixes her attention on a slab of smooth stone that stretches behind the fireplace. It groans when she mentally swings it open, revealing a dark shaft behind.

Lenny gapes at the shadowed passageway. 'Holy shit,' he murmurs. 'So this how you escaped?'

Death shifts closer. The cramped space can hardly fit the small, spiraling staircase that descends into total darkness.

Lenny sticks his head through the open doorway to peer down the stairs, and the look on Blair's face suggests she is contemplating pushing him.

'Yes,' the Tele admits begrudgingly. 'The stairs lead to the tunnels beneath the castle. These hidden passageways were built into most of the larger rooms and were used as an escape route — back when Ilya was weak and on the verge of being conquered,' she educates flippantly. 'Now they are hardly used, just like the tunnels.'

Lenny nods slowly. 'So, how does it—?'

Blair sighs as though she doesn't love proving that she's smarter than him. 'This is the flue.' She points to the hidden shaft. 'It is quite large to accommodate the many fireplaces littered throughout the castle. Adjacent rooms also have access to this stairwell, and it's completely enclosed until dropping into a tunnel.'

The Imperial pulls his head from the fireplace. 'Despite your condescending tone,' he mutters, 'that was actually very informative. Thank you.'

It was. Death quite enjoyed the lesson. She is always looking for something to learn, even in her old age (which a lady would never reveal,of course).

'So—' Lenny continues, folding his arms over that wrinkled uniform '—how did you find out about this? I knew there were all sorts of secret passages in the castle — everyone does — but no one really knows where half of them are anymore.'

'My father told me,' Blair answers curtly. 'As a general, he obviously knows what escape routes are in the castle.'

'So he told you how to sneak out?' Lenny smiles in that boyish way. Mara finds it rather adorable — then she supposes that the formidable Death shouldn't use such words. She has a reputation to uphold. 'I didn't realize your pops was so easygoing.'

'He's not,' the Tele corrects hotly. 'But even he realized that I might need an escape every once in a while.'

That seems to mellow the Imperial. 'From your mother?'

Blair glares at him, teetering on that irreversible something, remember. She doesn't deign to say a word before grabbing a dusty lantern from the mantel. Then, with a smug smile that looks surprisingly difficult to summon, the Tele ducks into the dark passageway.

'Blair!' Lenny scrambles after her. 'You can't leave.'

Her patronizing response is a distant echo. 'Try to stop me, gingersnap.'

Mara watches the Imperial tip his head toward the ceiling, as one might when praying for strength to whoever will listen. 'Fine,' he calls. 'I'm coming with you.'

'Plagues help me,' she mutters.

'I heard that.'

'I know.'

Their voices fade into the darkness, leaving Death to her own devices. Though intrigued by this defiant adventure, Mara hardly feels the need to endure the journey there with them. She has already walked that long path once before, and if she weren't already dead, she might not have survived their incessant arguing.

No, Death will simply meet them there. She is living (metaphorically speaking), breathing (again, not quite) power. Of course, outside the Mors, she is limited. But the simple willing of time and space to appear beside a bickering pair of souls is certainly doable.

Now, with the time she will save not walking, Mara decides to join the festivities. Contrary to popular belief, Death is quite capable of having fun. She can regularly be found among a grove of trees within the Mors, swapping stories of the living for gossip about the souls.

But tonight, Mara must be discreet. She never imagined there would come a time when she didn't wish to be seen. But the king now knows more about her than any other being – a horrifyingly invigorating thought. So, regrettably, Death believes it best to avoid him until she devises a better plan.

How very mature of her.

Upon entering the crowded ballroom, Mara becomes immediately aware of how underdressed she is for the occasion. Her dark cloak is plain and worn in the face of such finery. Of course, Death is not opposed to silk and frills – she is a woman who appreciates pretty things, after all – but her occupation demands a certain dullness. Souls would hardly take her seriously in a pretty pink.

Hmm.

Perhaps that is precisely why she should don such femineity. Mara already earns a wide array of disbelief and demeaning jokes from most men she drags to the Mors. But the eventual look of horror — usually following the acceptance that, holy shit, this really is Death — is well worth the wait. And a delicate ensemble would make that moment all the more delicious.

It is a relief to be unseen by those in sparkling jewels and glittering gowns, as Mara would turn every head in her gloomy attire. Though, there is one within this throng of gossipers who could undoubtedly recognize the face of Death (again, how strangely exhilarating), and he sits stiffly upon a throne at the ballroom's opposite end.

Kitt Azer is a creature of habit, Mara is beginning to realize. He may be king, but he much prefers his study to peacocking before a court. His face remains impressively blank — an oddity for one usually so expressive. But this is likely due to Death's impromptu visit. The king's mind must be reeling behind those green eyes. And Mara must avoid them for the evening.

(She finds this objective oddly disappointing.)

Mara slinks along the room's perimeter, clinging to the wall. Laughter echoes all around from those convinced this Paedyn Gray will fail tremendously. Though Death does not know this woman, she grows rather irked on her behalf. It is a rampant commonality, this feeling of being underestimated.

So Mara waits. This woman seems worth it. And when the

grand pair of doors swings open, every head turns to behold the belittled.

Paedyn Gray strides into the room, bloody and triumphant.

Several strands of her silver hair are stained scarlet. Cuts pepper her muddy skin, displayed beneath the torn clothing clinging to her.

She places a broken crown atop her head.

A queen to be. An underestimation to be reckoned with.

Mara was wrong. She does indeed know this woman.

In the Purging Trials — a stab wound to her abdomen.

Death was there.

In the Scorches — exhausted and on the brink of consciousness.

Death was there.

In a dark sewer — swelling with water and drowning out hope.

Death was there.

This soul is no stranger to ruin.

Mara has been summoned to her side more times than she can remember. And yet, this woman always manages to live.

It's astonishing, really. Death has begun to dread the day this soul finally loses her grip on the tightrope she has dangled from for so long.

Now she has a name.

Paedyn Gray — Death's most elusive soul.

It glows a bright silver in her chest, shimmering like the hair above, now stained with blood.

Pure. Fierce.

Every soul tells a story, and hers is riddled with perseverance.

Mara watches her stride towards the king.

Yes, she looks forward to meeting Paedyn Gray again.

In this life and the next.

CHAPTER 10

Mara

Lenny fails to notice Death's sudden presence beside him on Loot's uneven cobblestone.

She finds herself a bit disappointed by this – Mara was hoping her absence was felt – though unsurprised. Alas, the Imperial is far too engrossed by the Tele accompanying him. He watches Blair take in the moonlit slums, disdain carving a path through her stony expression.

This does not sit well with Lenny.

'If you hate the slums so much,' he remarks curtly, 'why did you want to come here?'

Blair flashes him a look of disgust. 'I don't hate the slums.'

'Oh, really?' The Imperial chuckles dryly. 'Everything about you says otherwise.'

'I've pretended to hate it here,' she snaps. 'Even now, I'm

only angry because I never got to have this.'

'This?' Lenny gestures towards the street, littered with meandering souls. 'Blair, these people would give anything to have what you were handed.'

Mara, who knows most things and feels a great deal more, adamantly agrees with this.

'You think I don't know that?' The words aren't nearly as biting as she intends. 'Still, I would give anything to live how I please, love who I please. But I can't, and I don't, because I'm trapped.'

The Imperial stares at her. Death does the same beside him.

'Blair—'

A looming figure steps before them, blocking the path.

The man can't be any older than Lenny, though it is clear which one of them was blessed with a towering physique – in Mara's trivial opinion. His broad shoulders lift with each breath, muscles straining beneath his black tunic and vest. Moonlight sharpens his cheekbones and highlights the scar slicing through his lips. A silver streak mars his wavy black hair – and, distantly, Death thinks one of his arms is the size of her leg.

Lenny clears his throat, perhaps intending to take charge as the Imperial in this situation. But Blair beats him to it, sounding rather bored, in fact. 'Can we help you?'

'Yes.' The stranger's deep voice chills the air. 'I've been looking for you, Blair Archer.'

'Damn, he even sounds cool,' Lenny mutters in awe.

Death's lips twitch, though the gesture is seen by no one. Curious, she takes a peek at this man's soul. The dull orange she's greeted with is surprising.

Blair looks magnificently unimpressed, so her Imperial attempts to follow suit. 'Look,' Lenny starts, 'you seem lovely, but we have somewhere to be. So, if you don't mind—'

An invisible force knocks him aside, suddenly.

Mara's brows lift in surprise (this is a rare show of expression from her).

Lenny stumbles back, nearly losing his footing, as the man says, 'I'm not here for you.'

Another Tele, then. This should be rather interesting.

Blair stands her ground, as condescending as ever. 'If it's money you want, I suggest trying to rob someone else.'

'Not money.' The man's menacing form towers over her. 'But a debt is owed.'

'Blair,' Lenny warns as he scrambles back to her side. 'Don't do anything—'

'And what are you going to do about it?'

'—stupid,' the Imperial finishes weakly.

The man's nostrils flare in response to Blair's condescension. For a moment, his dark eyes seem to cut right through to her swirling soul. And within that pocket of time, Death thinks he might just walk away.

Then she hears a soft gasp.

Mara's gaze flicks back to Blair, finding her still wearing that stony facade. But her skin begins to pale; her eyes water.

Lenny swallows. 'Blair?'

A sickening gasping sound slips past her lips. She lifts a hand to her neck.

The stranger is choking her.

And yet, she refuses to break the man's stare.

Death can feel it in her chest, the hum of a life thread splintering, right where a beating heart would be. She feels drawn to Blair, as she does when an endangered soul is in her vicinity. A connection is being forged between them, something tangible and final.

'Blair!' Lenny is shaking her shoulders now. Then he turns to shout his desperation at the man. 'Why are you doing this? Let her go!'

With a thought from the stranger, Lenny is thrown back several feet to collide with a merchant's cart. He curses, crashing into a display of fabrics before toppling to the ground. Groaning, the Imperial braces his palms against the cobblestone to push himself into a more dignified position.

A rasped cry has him stiffening.

Mara turns to find Blair hovering several feet above the ground, struggling against a fellow Tele's power.

'You killed her.' The man looks up at Blair's hanging body, his hand outstretched. 'You used this very power to drive a branch through her back. Her back!'

Hmm. He, too, must wish to avenge the mysterious, murdered friend.

Lenny limps towards him. Death is unsure as to what he could possibly do, and the Imperial looks to be thinking the same. Yet, he does not stop.

'She is gone because of you,' the man breathes. And despite the darkness, the grief that consumes him is visible. It dwells in his hollow gaze, his trembling voice.

He didn't just know this woman. He loved her.

It all makes sense to Mara now. Loving is the gravest danger one can put themselves in. Those you hold dear will inevitably slip from between your grasping fingers.

Death isn't pessimistic. She is experienced.

It is revenge – an inescapable blight – that drives the stranger to hurl his lover's killer into the wall of a crumbling building.

'Blair!'

She does not move at the sound of Lenny's cry.

He runs towards her, limping as fast as he can. Death follows with the Tele in tow, now plucking a small knife from his belt. The Imperial can do nothing to stop this vindictive stranger as he sends that blade cutting through the dense darkness.

A heartbeat later (Mara assumes) it tears through the flesh of Blair's shoulder, right below the birthmark hidden by her tunic (Death only knows this intimate detail because she caught Lenny's gaze tracing it the night before). The Imperial trips in his haste to reach her, skidding to a stop beside her slumped form. She stirs in pain, her face pale and peppered with cuts.

Lenny drops to his knees.

She is troublesomely limp against the wall – though, still alive. Death's connection to her has not yet fully formed.

'You're okay,' he reassures, likely to himself. 'You—'

Steel sings from behind, cutting through the Imperial's words when the stranger pulls a sword from its sheath. 'You killed her,' he growls. 'Now I will kill you.'

'No!'

Lenny stands to his feet, looking ready to throw himself at the towering man.

Perhaps their reaching souls aren't entirely absurd, Death thinks reluctantly. This Hyper seems ready to risk his life for the one he has deemed a Tele tyrant. How annoyingly fascinating.

The stranger raises a hand, intending to throw Lenny from his feet.

The Imperial braces himself for another mental shove – one that never comes.

Instead, it is this new Tele who is thrown backward.

The pommel of his sword sinks into the soft skin beneath his eye, hard enough to promise a bruise. Mara watches him hit the ground with a thud. Disturbing the darkness, his large body sprawls atop the cobblestone.

Lenny stares down at his hands in astonishment.

'It was me, idiot,' Blair pants, wiping blood from her nose.

'Right.' Lenny crouches beside her. 'Of course it was.'

She lacks the strength to roll her eyes at him, but the sentiment is there. Breathing heavy, she calls out to the Tele now picking himself up off the ground. 'This is between you and me. Leave gingersnap out of it.'

The Imperial winces slightly. 'Well, that was almost really touching—'

'Shut up,' Blair rasps.

They do make the most interesting pair.

Obediently pressing his lips together, Lenny helps pull her into a more comfortable position before the Tele is standing over them once again. Mara leans against the wall, having found the perfect vantage point to continue observing the chaos. Her services may yet be needed.

The stranger's eye waters, but the gaze he pins on Blair is unwavering. 'If that is your final wish, so be it.'

Moonlight glints off the steel sword. It arcs through the air, flashing above them.

Blair doesn't move. She only stares up at the face of revenge.

Death feels her lifeline grow taut. The Mors will happily welcome another soul.

But it is the Imperial, presumably weak and woefully bearing the brunt of every joke, who dives in front of the swinging blade.

'Get out of the way!'

It's the stranger who bellows this after barely being able to redirect the steel. Lenny, his eyes still squeezed shut, is practically sitting in Blair's lap in a bewildering attempt to shield her body. Slowly, he peeks up at the fuming man. That gleaming tip of steel is now steadily aimed at the Imperial's heart.

'I said,' the man growls in frustration, 'get out of the way.'

'No.' Lenny swallows. 'Death is too kind for her.'

Mara tilts her head. Is she too kind for Blair?

She does not think too long on this. Death is simply pleased to be included in the conversation.

'You want her to suffer, just like you're suffering,' the Imperial continues in a rush. 'And she already is. Hell, she's stuck with me every day.' The man doesn't lower his sword. 'If you kill her, she will be free from this life she hates more than anything. And besides,' he breathes, 'I didn't know Adena personally, but I think she would have objected to you killing people on her behalf.'

Adena.

Death remembers the name of every soul she has ever gathered. Now she knows exactly of whom they speak.

Mara recalls scooping the vibrant soul from a stretch of bloody sand. She was quiet, Adena, in a way that suggested she often wasn't when alive. But most memorable of all, she was not afraid. Peace itself was relieved to find her.

'Let Blair live,' the Imperial murmurs. He holds the man's gaze. 'It's the most pain you could offer her.'

A long moment passes.

Death thinks fondly of that sunny soul.

There is a sudden flash of steel. The sword drops from Lenny's throat.

'For Adena,' the man chokes.

And then he disappears into the night.

Lenny is much sturdier than Death previously gave him credit for.

He carries Blair with little sign of strain, her head lolling against his starchy shoulder.

'Almost there,' he murmurs.

'Almost where, Lenny?' The Tele's question is more slurred than assertive.

'No insulting nickname?' He picks up his pace (Death is then forced to do the same), thoroughly jostling the wounded girl in his arms. 'You really are hurt.'

Blair tries again, these words more biting. 'Where are you taking me?'

Mara has been wondering just that. She looks to Lenny, awaiting his answer.

'To my house.'

'You mean,' Blair begins hoarsely, 'you live with a bunch of sweaty Imperials by choice?'

Death follows her escort around a corner as he says, 'Those sweaty Imperials are worth the luxury of living in a castle.'

Blair groans with as much scorn as she can muster. 'Yes, but you have a curfew. Do you get tucked into bed, too?'

'I know you're making fun of me right now, but I would not object to a nightly tuck in.'

'Of course you wouldn't,' Blair mumbles.

They turn another corner and—

Death comes to an abrupt halt. In another lifetime, her heart would have been pounding.

Mara drags her gaze over the cluster of gnarled trees that crowd a rickety house. Their branches are intertwined, weaving around one another in an infinite embrace.

This is that patch of earth – the one Death has been avoiding since her return to Ilya. Those trees were once thriving, so tall they seemed to scrape the sky with their branches. Now they curl with time, decay from the horrors they have witnessed.

But the flimsy home Lenny strides towards is mercifully unfamiliar.

Mara forces her feet forward. She stops before the worn door. A pile of sand adorns the step beneath.

Death refuses to feel. Just as the living assume of a heinous creature such as she.

'Whose house is this?'

The Imperial kindly answers Blair's question. 'It's mine now. But Ma and I used to live here. Now—' he sets the limp Tele down '—can you stand for a second?'

'Yes, I know how to stand, gingersnap.'

'Ah. Sounds like someone is already feeling better.'

Lenny tugs at a faded pink ribbon around his neck. Mara, to her dismay, had failed to notice it peeking out from beneath the collar of his uniform. An iron key hangs at the end of it, intricate and decorated with swirling metal. After shoving it hastily into a lock, he then shoulders open the door.

'Home sweet home,' Lenny sighs.

He moves to slide an arm around Blair. 'Don't,' she snarls. 'I don't need your help.'

Palms raised, the Imperial steps aside. 'Suit yourself.'

The Tele lifts her chin. This must make her terribly dizzy, because she immediately stumbles into the doorframe.

Lenny clears his throat. 'Sure you don't need—?'

'Just get me inside,' Blair seethes.

He swiftly obeys, wrapping a hesitant arm around his assignment's waist. She leans heavily on him as they step into what is generously deemed a home. It's a glorified shack, really, with its slatted roof and lack of furniture.

Mara surveys the shadowed space and finds only an inkling of relief.

No piece of the past lingers here.

'Where is your mother now?' Blair asks, easing herself onto a stiff cot decorating the floor.

Lenny visibly shudders as he crouches before her. 'It feels wrong to think of her as "Mother". Seems so cold and formal.'

'It is,' she responds dully. 'Not all of us are blessed with a "Ma".'

'Right.' He nods slowly. 'I guess I'm pretty lucky, then.

But Ma is in Dor now, sheltering Elites whose powers are too weak to safely remain in Ilya. Because of multiple Ordinary ancestors,' he clarifies.

Death thoroughly enjoys talk of these Elites and Ordinaries. It is quite fun, as though she is the only one laughing at an untold joke.

Lenny rifles through the bundle of clothing beside his bleary-eyed assignment on the cot. 'Okay, nothing is broken, right? I feel like you would be even less pleasant if that were the case.'

'No. Nothing is broken.'

Hmm. Mara is a bit disappointed by her lack of retort. In fact, upon further study, it seems the Tele is rather defeated. If Death were to wager a guess – and, of course, she will – it would be that Blair Archer is unused to pain. She doesn't let anyone get close enough to hurt her. That borrowed ability is the only defense she knows, and when that is stripped away, she is weak. Or rather, just as she was meant to be.

'Good,' Lenny says, relieved. 'Now, I just need to bandage you up until we can discreetly get a Healer to your room. I'm not really sure how to go about doing that, but—'

'Are you capable of thinking these thoughts inside your head?' Blair grinds out between her teeth. 'Because you're making mine pound harder.'

'Ah, yes, let's start there.'

He is completely unbothered by her biting words. This only annoys Blair further.

His fingers brush her forehead, startling the Tele. 'What the hell are you doing?'

'Trying to help,' he says slowly. Hesitantly, he swipes a strand of tangled hair from her eyes. 'There. Now I can see that gash on your temple.'

Mara takes a seat on the lumpy cot. They may be here awhile.

'Why are you helping me?' Blair demands.

Lenny tears a strip of fabric from the pile of abandoned clothing. 'Aside from it kind of being my job?' His eyes flick over a glaring Blair. 'Why didn't you fight that Tele?'

She grinds her teeth together. Death can hear it. 'I did.'

'No,' the Imperial corrects. 'You didn't – not really. I could hear your heart. It only slowed, like . . . like you—'

'Accepted my fate,' Blair finishes curtly. Her voice is steady. 'That man is the second person who wants me dead for what I did in that arena. Maybe it's time to admit they have a point.'

Lenny stares at her. The moon slips through those slits in the roof, trickling dull light across his face. He wears the type of look that begs to be analyzed, picked apart until each layer of emotion is on display. But even Mara does not know what it is he's thinking, feeling – is or isn't.

'Are you just going to let me bleed out over here?' Blair blurts harshly.

Her words cut through the concern on the Imperial's face. 'Right.' He clears his throat and lifts that strip of cloth to Blair's forehead.

'Is that—' a look of repulsion pinches her features '—sand?'

'Oh, yeah.' After wrapping her head with the makeshift bandage, Lenny ties a knot against her hair. 'I just recently got back from the Scorches.'

'What?'

'I was a part of that Resistance that failed,' he says casually. 'I even rescued Pae from the Enforcer and took them to Dor. But then they vanished from our camp – it was a whole thing.' He sighs. 'That's why I came back to Ilya, actually. I was going to smuggle Paedyn out of the kingdom before I found out Kitt had no intention of killing her.'

Hmm. Death had not expected that. Over the years, she has collected more than a few martyrs and radicals and those ravenous for justice. But Lenny does not look like the rest. No, he is still a boy with a heart much too soft – a luxury that revolution cannot afford. Kindness is rarely jarring enough to instill change, you see, so cruelty is often justified by pure intentions.

Casually, the Imperial lifts that worn tunic again to rip more fabric from its hem.

Blair stares at the sandy garment, her voice lethal. 'Are these the sweaty clothes you wore in the Scorches?'

Lenny has the audacity to snort. 'I tell you I was a Resistance member, and that is the first thing you ask?'

'I don't care about your treason,' she declares. 'It's honestly unsurprising, considering you're a Hyper and your best friend is an Ordinary. What I do care about, however, is your filthy clothing on my open wound.'

He winces. 'It's not ideal, I'll admit. But I don't have any other clothes.'

'I could strangle you.'

'Save your energy.' Lenny leans in to examine the slice on her forearm. 'Besides—' he flashes her a smile she happily scowls at '—I did just save your life.'

He had.

Death notes that this does not sit well with Blair.

'Did you mean what you said?' she asks, her tone indifferent. 'About how me living is more torturous than Death?'

Mara perks up at such a direct mention.

When Lenny glances at his assignment, moonlight splatters his face with pale freckles of its own. 'Was it true?'

Blair seems to be at war with herself.

'I wanted to be a baker,' she finally blurts.

Hmm. Yet another unexpected discovery this evening. Unlike Lenny, the Tele seems entirely too cutting and cruel for such an admission of self.

Wisely, Lenny does not laugh. 'What?'

'Since we are admitting things,' she forces out, 'you should know that I always wanted to be a baker.'

The Imperial blinks. This is then followed by the predicted laughter. 'I'm sorry, I just can't imagine you wanting to make anyone feel warm and fuzzy inside.'

'Well, there are only about four occupations you can have in this Plague-forsaken kingdom,' she retorts, though the venom in her voice begins to fade. 'And when I was a little girl, baking was the only thing in my life I could control. Every measurement, every spice – it was mine to manipulate.'

Death can understand this. In another life, she, too, yearned for control. Now Mara is at the mercy of the Mors.

Lenny tenderly wraps the gash beneath her torn tunic sleeve. 'So . . .' He sounds hesitant, as though at any moment, Blair might run away from this sudden vulnerability. 'Why are you not a baker, then?'

She exhales slowly. 'My mother wanted a boy – a strong male to take my father's place as general one day.' Both Mara and the Tele roll their eyes. 'So, from the moment of my birth, I was a disappointment. Mother knew I would have to work extra hard to earn my father's position, because for whatever reason, being a woman is perceived as a disadvantage.'

Death is beginning to understand this difficult human – perhaps even like her.

Lenny holds his assignment's gaze, silently urging this spilling of honesty from her lips. 'By the age of four,' she continues curtly, 'Mother had me training for half the day. My power was the only thing she'd ever really liked about me. So, she forced me to become what she never could be – lethal, harsh, a condescending bitch. Or so I've heard.'

A shadowed smile lifts the Imperial's lips. 'We are both

allowed an insulting nickname.'

Blair smothers him with a flat look. 'Anyway, it became Mother's sole mission to mold me into her perfect creation. She taught me to intimidate, never show fear. The princes were viewed as my competition, an obstacle I needed to conquer in everything.' She pauses, looking annoyed by her own unsolicited admission. 'And I couldn't help but resent them. Not because my mother wanted me to, but because they were allowed to *live*. They had so much power, and yet, the boys got to be just that – boys.'

She is tearing at the skin on her palm now. 'I was never allowed friends, or fun, or food that I enjoyed. My life was not my own. And when I grew tired of forcing the same tasteless slop down my throat, I decided to make that the one thing I could control. I would sneak into the kitchen, stealing spices, fruit, anything I could get my hands on.'

'I wondered why Gail seemed to know you so well,' Lenny murmurs.

'She knew I was taking her supplies.' The Tele almost smiles at the thought. 'And yet, she never tried to stop me. Maybe she realized it was my escape from the callous girl Mother required I be. But then—' her voice grows chilled '—the sergeant caught me.'

'Sergeant,' Lenny echoes in understanding. 'So, it's your ma – sorry, mother.'

'She hates when I call her that, which is precisely why I

do,' Blair says simply. 'It's fitting, though — she spews more orders than my father ever has. So, when she discovered I had a passion that didn't benefit my fate as a general, she declared that baking was nonsense and ordered I never do it again. Continuing my family's legacy is all I'm meant for.'

Again, Death feels a pang of sympathy.

Lenny leans in, listening closely. Mara is surprised he can go so long without speaking. 'So, I made a deal with her that day,' Blair continues. 'If I won the Purging Trials, bringing more honor to our family than any general could, she would have to let me go.' She looks down at the angry skin on her palm. 'That was four years ago. And I spent every day after becoming the harshest, most lethal version of myself.'

'You had to win,' the Imperial murmurs. 'It makes sense now. But . . . why didn't you just run away?'

'I was young,' she retorts. 'I knew Mother would find me and call off our deal. But now . . . I have nothing to lose.' Her words are clipped. 'In those Trials, it was my life I was playing for. And if I won, I wouldn't have to live under the sergeant's control or the king's command. I could start over — be who I want, who I would have been before Mother made me this way.'

It is like looking in a mirror, Mara realizes, regrettably. Without ever seeing her, this girl knows Death more intimately than most. For they both burn with a passion that Fate laughs at.

Words continue to pour from Blair, threatening to drown

her. 'So when I killed that girl in the Bowl – Adena – I thought it would be all worth it in the end. I was supposed to win those Purging Trials. I had calculated my score, knew that if I finished that maze first, I would be free.'

Lenny hangs his head. 'But the Resistance attacked.'

Yes, Mara did remember collecting the sea of limp souls from that sandy arena. They were all quite content to be dead, she recalls. For most possessed a certain calmness that only accompanies purpose. Hope.

'And there was no winner for the sixth ever Purging Trials,' Blair muses. 'Mother refused to hold up her end of the bargain, so it was all for nothing. All the malice I met the world with, all the blood I spilt in the arena.' Her voice sounds oddly strained. 'That was my first deliberate kill. I really thought she was a criminal. But Adena's death didn't even let me live. So, yes,' she states plainly. 'What you said to the Tele was true.'

A stiff silence swells between them.

For the first time, Death feels as though she should not be intruding on this moment.

The pale moonlight peeking down on the tense scene paints Lenny's lashes silver. Blair must notice this too, because she is staring rather intently at him. That would be a first.

'So now you have nothing to say?' she finally spits.

The Imperial smiles thinly. '"*We are made this way.*" That is what you said to me about . . . well, bitches. And I think I understand that now.'

He looks at Blair, as though this is his first time truly seeing her. Mara is quietly envious — she has never been on the other side of such a stare. Not on this side of eternity.

The Tele nods distantly. 'My mother was made too. With a weak power, she was forced to feign strength. It's why she hates me for wanting to waste mine on passion.'

'I'm sorry,' Lenny offers slowly. 'About all of it. I'm sorry you had to go through that.'

His words only remind Blair to slam that stony facade back into place. She straightens with a wince. 'I don't need your pity.'

'No, you don't,' he agrees. 'That's why I'm offering you my help instead.' The Imperial nods, his mind elsewhere. 'You're going to get out of here. And I won't let my reputation get in the way of that.'

'But—' Blair's facade is crumbling again '—you were going to find a way that didn't make you look even more weak—'

'Thanks, yeah, I remember,' Lenny cuts in swiftly. 'But that attack earlier . . . That was a reminder.' He swallows. 'It's time to cut the shit and face it — I will always be weak. You were right. No one expects me to actually protect you.'

There is a forced tone of hilarity in the words, one Death is certain he has honed over the years. He is likely used to diminishing himself before others get the chance, hiding behind his humor. It's a sad cycle, Mara decides.

'Fine.' Blair folds her arms, wincing yet again. 'Then I'll teach you how to be powerful.'

The Imperial finds this funny. 'Shit, are you being nice to me? How hard did you hit your head?'

'I can demonstrate with your skull.'

'Look—' Lenny lifts his hands defensively '—I appreciate the shockingly kind offer, but I'm a Hyper. "Powerful" just isn't a word that applies to me.'

'That's because you're only relying on your ability,' the Tele drawls lazily. 'Real power resides in how you're perceived. It's all an act.'

'And you?' the Imperial asks slowly. 'Are you all an act?'

Blair is drenched in moonlight when she lifts her chin. 'The act is all I've ever known.'

Yes, Death decides.

It is like looking in a mirror.

CHAPTER 11

A row of vials lines the edge of my desk. Each one is filled with a heinous assortment of herbs that I am expected to swallow every three hours. Eli, more somber than usual but as insistent as ever, promised a stern scolding if he returned to find his tonics untouched. Then he drifted distractedly from my study, scribbling into his booklet.

It has been less than twenty-four hours since Paedyn returned from that first Trial, wearing a bloody crown and displaying her wounds.

Less than twenty-four hours since the several glasses of champagne I guzzled while awaiting her, trying to quiet the noise in my head.

Less than twenty-four hours since Death showed her face, tugging at my weary soul.

I rub at my bleary eyes. They hardly shut last night, not when every shadow could be Death's. Even now, I flick my gaze over the study in search of that chestnut hair. But not for the reason most glance over their shoulder, wondering if it is Death's gaze they feel on the back of their neck. Fear of one's fate is what makes Mara so elusive. Some are obsessed with finding her before she finds them.

But it is not fear that drives me. It is the truth.

Even fewer hours have separated me from my first exploration of Mother's room since her death. Father never let me within ten feet of it, as if my presence alone would mar her memory. And perhaps, for once, his cruelty was warranted. It was my life that brought about Iris's death all those years ago.

Her bedroom was untouched, kept company only by a thick layer of dust. The jewelry box on her bedside table was unassuming. Though, the promise of tracing a ring that once clutched my mother's finger, or a necklace that hugged her closely, had me lifting the lid.

But the love notes I found inside did not display my father's bold handwriting. No, they were inked with looping letters and a devotion Edric Azer wasn't capable of.

I would know that curling penmanship by feel alone.

My mother was having an affair with the king's Mind Reader. With *my* Mind Reader.

Even the shiest whisper of an heir's illegitimacy can crumble a kingdom. And if I am a bastard, my real father is all that stands between me and my rule.

I drum my fingers against the chipped edge of my desk.

Mara has been avoiding me. And seeing that she is, in fact, Death, I should feel relieved. But between my fourth and fifth flute of champagne yesterday evening, I realized that her strange attachment to my soul could be useful.

Death knows the dead – *is* the dead.

With a sigh, I pull the gilded crown from my head. It would feel odd, wearing it as I reach for the silver letter opener hidden beneath strewn sheets of parchment. I'm not sure if what I'm about to do is brave, benevolent, or brutal. It's rather desperate, actually. Perhaps even teetering on the edge of something crazed and familiar.

But my forced fits of coughing aren't drawing her out. It seems she needs something more convincing. Something closer to Death herself.

I unsheathe the thin blade. It's dull, which provides an inkling of comfort. Though, that only makes piercing my skin all the more difficult.

I rest the point above my heart. Take a deep breath. Impale the threads of my tunic. Push until I prick the skin beneath. Farther still and blood blooms. Pain sears beneath the blade's persistence—

'What are you doing?'

Mara has arrived.

I've drawn Death from the shadows.

The lack of emotion on her face clashes with the veiled urgency in her voice. She's draped in her usual black attire – tunic, pants, cloak. The auburn hair I've searched for falls effortlessly into the hood at her back.

'Summoning you,' I answer truthfully. 'I wasn't sure it would work.'

'If you ask for Death, I answer.' Her eyes flick to the patch of dark blood staining my navy tunic. 'Your soul has already been marked. A blade to the heart is only begging me to steal it.'

'I'm not trying to die,' I say quickly. 'I'm only trying to get your attention.'

'You have my attention because you are dying.'

'Fine.' The word is curt. I pretend my compliance is conditional, due only because it is what she wishes to hear. But it is so much worse – I believe her. I'm afraid Death herself can be trusted to know the imminence of mine. 'So, help me before you steal my soul away.'

A shadow of surprise crosses her face. 'You really aren't afraid of me, are you?'

I set the letter opener back on the desk, careful not to drip blood onto my notes. 'You don't look like something I should be afraid of.'

'No.' She tilts her head. 'Not in this form.'

I don't dwell on her words, because I wish for my lack of

fear to remain. 'Running from Death only wastes your life,' I murmur. 'I would rather face you head-on.'

'Hmm.' She weighs my words carefully. 'You Azers are just as bold as I remember.'

'So you do remember the Azers?' I inquire quickly. 'All of them?'

'Some more than others.' Emotion flashes in her eyes. 'But, yes, I remember every soul I drag to the Mors.'

'The Mors,' I repeat, chewing on the foreign word. 'What is that?'

'It is where the dead reside.'

'Can the living go there?' I ask, sounding very much like the mad king I once was.

The corner of her mouth curls into a soft smile. 'The Mors is not a place that is found, or conquered, or coveted. It does not exist on your plane. Life may not cross over into Death's territory.'

I hold her gaze. 'But could I?'

That placid expression of hers never budges. 'Is that what you want my help with?'

'I need to speak with my mother.' The words spew from me, laced with desperation. 'I need to discover the truth about something, and she is the only one who can tell me. It is imperative that I speak with her. If I can go to the Mors—'

'Iris Azer.'

I fall silent at the name. Mara speaks it as though she is

reminiscing on a distant memory.

'I haven't checked on her in at least a decade,' she utters evenly. 'She was one of the easy souls.'

My throat bobs. 'Let me see her. Please.'

Death eyes me for a long moment. 'I don't usually speak to the living about the afterlife they will face.'

'Then why are you here?' I retort breathlessly. 'Why come to Ilya and haunt me? I'm still a living soul, after all.' I run a hand through my hair, wincing at the shallow wound on my chest. 'Why waste your time on someone you can't steal away just yet?'

A faint line forms between her brows, a physical crack in her stoic facade. 'Is Death not allowed to wonder about life? Stalk it, even?' Her gaze darkens. 'Just because I am Death, it does not mean I fail to feel.'

I'm surprised by the pang of guilt that accompanies her words. 'I'm sorry. I . . . I don't know anything about Death – you.' I shut my eyes with a sigh. 'I don't know anything about you.'

Mara stares at me long enough to catch one of my genuine coughs. It's more of a rasp, really, but I swallow the burning in my throat before it can swell.

I watch as Death's gaze shifts from me to the row of vials across my desk. 'Those won't help you.'

'I figured.'

'You cannot cheat Death.'

'I wouldn't dare try.'

'No, you wouldn't,' she agrees. 'But I could.'

My pounding heart quickens its pace. 'What?'

'You will need to die. Temporarily,' she adds. 'Like I said, only the dead can cross over.'

'And how do you know I'll only die temporarily?' It's a struggle to spit out the insanity. 'You can bring me back?'

Mara laces her fingers together. 'Contrary to popular belief, I am not responsible for choosing who goes to the Mors and when. I only bring them there when Life grows tired of them.' She drags her gaze over me. 'Your time will come. But it is not now.'

I stand from my seat, head spinning. 'So, how do I . . . die?'

'I can stop your heart,' she says plainly. 'Give you a proverbial push from the tightrope of life. I can pull you back after a few minutes, but time does not exist within the Mors, so it may feel as though you are there for a long while.'

The absurdity of each word is only rivaled by the fact that I'm speaking to Death herself. I pace atop the worn rug, treading a path behind my desk. This goes beyond the actions of a mad king, beyond any sane thought at all.

This is life and death and balancing somewhere in between.

But I would risk anything to speak with my mother one last time.

'What do you need me to do?' I ask sternly.

Mara shifts her gaze to the floor. 'Lie down and let me kill you.'

I appreciate her directness despite how threatening she sounds. So I stride past those worn armchairs and halt before the heated hearth. Glancing back at Death, I'm startled to find her right behind me. She still wears that flat expression, but I get the sense that her patience with me is wearing thin.

That realization has me swiftly flattening to the floor, where I watch her loom above. My voice sounds suddenly small. 'Why are you helping me?'

She kneels at my side. 'Curiosity.'

Any further questions are stifled when she places a hand on my chest. Her touch is cold, even through my bloodied tunic. But not in the way rain chills, or the stone walls cool in the winter. This is a lack of warmth, like a feeling of emptiness more than a sensation.

I suppress my shiver when she says, 'I don't have as much power outside the Mors. I usually remain within Death's territory. But in order to talk to you, the living, I crossed into this plane.'

'So, what are you saying?' I ask hesitantly.

She looks down at me with those eyes that seem to behold everything at once. 'To wake you up, I must remain here. That means you will explore the Mors alone.'

'Okay.' I swallow. 'As long as I'm alive for the ball.'

Slowly, she offers a final piece of instruction. 'When you find who you are looking for, touch them, and they will be able to see you.'

I'm thoroughly concerned before my heart even stutters.
It is a literal stalling of the organ.
What a strange sensation, life failing.
I gasp, but Death only pushes harder against my chest.
The world begins to blur at the edges, growing dark.
My heartbeat slows to a slothful pace.
Everything is slipping away.
I am drifting, drifting, drifting—
Dark.

CHAPTER 12
Mara

This is terribly reckless.

(But quite fun.)

Mara sits beside the unmoving king.

She killed him.

(Well, for now.)

Power strains beneath Death's skin. The Mors is her well, and when away from it, she starts to run dry.

But some part of her – perhaps the heart that aches to beat again – wants to appease the young Azer.

Terribly reckless, indeed.

Mara drags a cold finger across the king's knuckles. Then the stubbled curve of his jaw.

It is foreign, this feeling. Or rather, feeling anything at all.

Death does not touch the living. But his soul is so delicately in between.

A feeling begins to fester in her chest – something even more dangerous than she.

Hope.

Mara has experienced this horror firsthand. Like something pleasant that's a breath away from becoming painful. Water too cold, it burns. Fire too large, it consumes. Love too grand, it kills.

That is what Kitt Azer feels like.

An enticing devastation.

CHAPTER 13

Ritt

I wake with a strangled gasp.

My body feels stiff. I didn't think being dead would bring so much discomfort. It feels as though I've fallen through the floor of my study and slammed into the world below.

Is this what it feels like to be shoved from the proverbial tightrope by Death?

I stare up at the gray sky while I gulp down several shallow breaths. Thick fog whispers over me, tracing my figure like a pet playing with its food. I can sense a sort of hunger from the shifting dampness. This only compels my once-still heart to beat wildly.

The ground beneath me is cracked and dry, crumbling against my palms as I push myself into a sitting position. Sound is muffled within my ears. Blearily, I look down at the pale earth, tracing the web of cracks crawling in every direction. One is several inches wide and displaying a gaping nothingness below.

I should know better. My eager curiosity was one of the things Father hated most about me. And that, perhaps, is the reason I now indulge it.

My hand stretches towards that split in this strange world.

What is it that lies below the Mors? Another realm to be ruled by a stoic deity? Or maybe—

The earth rumbles beneath me.

I shove myself away when that crack in the ashen soil stretches and gapes. A guttural growl cuts through the pressure in my ears, reverberating from the ground that caves in beside me.

The impossibility of it all stuns me for a second too long. I'm slipping, sliding towards the ravenous earth that wishes to swallow me whole. A strained shout is coaxed from my throat when I stare into the nothingness reaching for me. My fingers claw at the crumbling ground, desperately trying to pull myself from the growing grave at my feet.

It seems the Mors feels cheated by my almost-death.

Wrenching myself free from the splitting soil, I struggle to my feet. My heart pounds in time to each of my strides. I sprint through the fog, throwing a glance over my shoulder.

The ground is caving in behind me.

Destruction is a step too slow, nipping at my heels. I

yell – for Death, some kinder deity – I'm not sure. But the earth is hungry for my soul and if it sinks its teeth into me, I may never return to the living.

My lungs burn.

The ground is cracking beneath my feet, splintering with each step—

I collide with something dense, hidden behind a wall of fog.

Something hits the ground with a thud at the same moment I do. My body aches, but panic has me scrambling backward on palms sinking into slimy moss. I stare wildly at the ground, waiting for it to devour me whole.

But it remains perfectly solid.

I shake my head at the blanket of fog nestling against this strange earth.

I don't understand. It was all just crumbling. Chasing me.

'H-hello?'

The hesitant voice drifts from the chalky air beside me. I look up to find a small woman squinting through the fog. Her hair is a tangled mess of gray, some of it torn from her scalp in clumps. The ragged clothes clinging to her are worn enough to display most of her wrinkled skin.

I clear my throat, unsure. 'Down here.'

The woman's eyes snap to mine, far clearer than I figured they would be. The sight of me has a wild grin spreading across her face. It grows into an eerie display of blackened gums and missing teeth.

'You can hear me?' she whispers in awe.

I stand to my feet swiftly. The look on her face displays a hunger that could rival the ravenous ground beneath. 'Yes?'

The woman cackles, and I take a step back at the crazed sound. 'I see you!' She practically sings out the words in a chilling tune. I begin pacing backward when she reaches gnarled hands towards me, grasping at the air where I was. 'You are my way out! Tell me how to get out!'

'No, you don't understand—'

'Get me out!' she screeches. Each demand is more earsplitting than the last. 'Get me out! Get me out! Get me out!'

I turn, poised to outrun this bewildering disaster too.

But what I find behind that curtain of fog has my feet fumbling.

Hundreds – *thousands* – of bodies fill the Mors. As far as the eye can see, souls mill aimlessly in every direction. Their mouths move, but only a haunting silence meets my ears. Some are haggard, others lost, most hysterical. They pass through one another like ghosts, never seeing or hearing those suffering with them.

This is eternal loneliness.

All the breath flees from my lungs.

So this is the afterlife I have to look forward to.

Bony fingers wrap around my bicep, startling me. The deranged woman is clawing at my skin with brittle nails. 'Help me! Take me with you!'

I tear out of her weak hold and run towards the throng of bodies.

I can't help her. I can't.

But that doesn't stop the frail woman from persistently chasing what she believes to be her salvation. It shouldn't be too difficult to lose the old woman, though, only one of us has to worry about dodging meandering souls.

I realize now that Mara's instructions were a veiled warning.

Be careful who you touch.

With that in mind, I weave through the bodies, elbows tucked firmly at my sides. Before me is a mass of wandering souls. Behind me is a crowing woman who is surprisingly agile for her age.

This close to the dead, I can see now that most move with a purpose. Dozens are knee-deep in a murky swamp ahead, digging in the muck as though some treasure lies within. Others are searching under every stone or scaling spindly trees.

Is it boredom or belief in something that has them scouring the Mors?

I turn towards a cluster of gaunt trees, picking up the pace when a shrieking plea echoes behind. Each labored breath only reminds me how out of shape Kai let me get while he was hunting down my betrothed.

Kai.

That is who I do all this for. Before we begin building our great legacy together, we need to ensure that no secrets can steal it away from us.

My boots sink into thick, black mud as I scan the faces surrounding me. Despite never meeting my mother, I can picture her clearly. Perhaps she has visited my dreams, conjured up from the few portraits Father occasionally let me see. So I search for her blond hair, hope to catch her blue gaze in the crowd.

I happily lean against the first gnarled tree I meet. It feels as though I have been running for hours, futilely searching for Iris Azer. Moss tickles the back of my neck, drooping from a twisted branch above. Still, I rest my head against the knotted trunk, discouraged.

Mara is going to pull me out of here any second, and I haven't even found—

A figure suddenly steps beside me.

I'm forced to stumble back before our arms brush, leaving me with yet another pleading soul to escape. I look up slowly. And a very hardened, spiteful, dead version of myself stares back.

This is not the Azer I was hoping to find.

Father looks up at the tree, clueless of my presence. Dark circles smudge the skin beneath his eyes. The blond hair we share is now thinning atop his head, or maybe I've just never seen him without a crown to cover it up. His gaze is distant as it roams over the branches. He looks like a man who lost the only thing keeping him sane – power.

Again, I know I shouldn't. But this time, it is not my insufferable curiosity that sways me.

I stretch a hand towards Father's shoulder.

I want him to need me. For once.

His green eyes slide to mine the moment my fingers fall from that bloody shirt he died in. 'Kitt?'

My voice is stubbornly even. 'Hello, Father.'

He looks me over with that steely gaze, sharp enough to cut. Just like he has my entire life, Father searches for flaws to exploit. 'You're dead? Already?' He shakes his head. 'I always knew you were too weak to rule.'

For once, I refuse to flee from his ire. 'No, Father, I'm not dead. Just visiting.'

His scoff is a familiar sound. 'Visiting? What the hell are you talking about?'

'Death – the woman who dragged you here – let me stop by to speak with my mother,' I inform.

And just like that, his entire demeanor shifts. I have just become useful to him. 'Iris,' he murmurs. 'Yes, help me find Iris.' His gaze grows wild; he plants shaking palms on the tree's trunk. 'Here. She has to be in here. Her voice . . . it's coming from the tree.'

I can't help but gape at him. Father's mind was always sharp, cruel – nothing like the unraveling mess before me. But it seems that Death changes a person.

'Help me get your mother out,' Father orders, sounding like his old self despite the sudden hysteria. 'Then we can all go home. You will take us home.'

My gaze is icy. Aiming such a pointed glare at the man I once lived to please feels equally wrong and cathartic. 'Tell me you need my help.'

Father doesn't bother looking at me. 'I need your help, Kitt. Now get us out of here.'

Despite the flippancy with which he says the words, I figured it would mean more hearing them from him. But the infatuation is gone, leaving only a man before me. A mediocre one at that.

I can't help but smile. 'I'm not taking you home.'

Father scowls at me. It's a look he only ever gave Kai. 'You will do as I say, boy.'

'No, I won't.' I take a slow step towards him. 'I worked so hard to impress you, earn your praise, because I thought you were doing something great. Something worth all the pain you put your sons through.' My voice wavers with emotion. 'But you were too obsessive to do anything great.'

Father barks out a laugh. 'Look in a mirror, Son. Your own obsession is what brought you here,' he taunts. 'You wanted to see me.'

'No—'

'Even now, you are consumed by trying to be better than me.' He stands a breath away now, like some cruel reflection of what I could become. 'But you will fail. Your weakness will be your undoing.'

'I will be stronger than you ever were!' I roar with a shove to his chest. 'My legacy will bury yours in the history books. I will become the greatness you never were.'

'You will remain exactly as you always have,' Father spits. 'A disappointment.'

My fist is suddenly clenched around the collar of his soiled tunic while the other pulls back to strike. Father seems to find his unfortunate position funny. 'Go on, Son,' he goads. 'Hit me. I dare you to actually do something that takes an inkling of strength.'

My throat bobs. I hesitate.

Another condescending laugh. 'A damn Ordinary killed me, and you can't even throw a punch!'

Still, my fist does not meet his face. I want to see the look in his eyes when I murmur, 'You can rot here knowing that I will never continue your mediocre plan for Ilya.' I pause, letting the words sink in. 'No, I am going to rule over every kingdom. And they will worship me like a god for the powers I give them.'

I watch with a smile as all the color drains from his face. 'Th-the Plague,' Father stutters. 'You wouldn't—'

'I *am*.' Every word is sharp. 'Your pride made you weak. There is no need to covet our power when I can rule over every kingdom it touches. So it is you, Father, who will be a disappointment in the shadow of my great legacy.'

I let my fist fly towards his face.

And then—

Dark.

My heart flutters back to life.

And I wake on the floor of my study with a choking gasp.

CHAPTER 14
Mara

The king is just barely alive when a swarm of Imperials come to collect him for the ball.

He is found, most unfortunately, still recovering on the floor of his study. A Healer is called to Kitt's side within a matter of moments, though he does little more than poke and prod at the protesting king.

Mara finds the whole display quite comical, really. When unable to rely on their ability to miraculously heal, these avowed physicians are rendered utterly useless. On second thought, perhaps Death finds this cynically sad.

Kitt all but commands every concerned face from the room and, with a quick glance at Mara, sets a steady pace towards the ballroom. Death considers his lingering gaze an invitation to accompany him, and who is she to deny the king?

The entourage stops before the ballroom's looming doors, where a servant hands Kitt (His Majesty to her – unlike Mara, who is enviously on a first-name basis with the king) a black suit coat to shrug on over his tunic (dark enough to disguise the splotch of blood that summoned Death to his study). That twining crown is back upon his golden hair, gleaming in the dull light. He is undeniably handsome, Mara thinks, because it is a fact, and is she not allowed to simply state the truth?

The king gestures for his throng of Imperials, and the paranoid Healer, to take a step back. Mara, for a reason unbeknownst to her, steps into the empty space beside him. With his gaze still pinned on the closed doors, Kitt murmurs beneath his breath, 'We are waiting for Paedyn.'

Death, though no one can see her but the king, does not look at him either. 'Your betrothed.'

He is quiet for a long moment. 'I can't imagine what else you've heard around the castle.'

'Your Majesty?' the Healer inquires. 'Did you say something?'

'No, Eli.' Kitt's voice is even but not unkind. 'And be sure to keep your distance tonight. My brother will ask questions if you are following me around all evening.'

'Yes, Your Majesty.'

The silence resumes, only to be shattered by the distant tapping of heels. Paedyn Gray soon fills the space on Kitt's opposite side, draped in a sheet of silver.

'You look lovely,' he says to her steadily.

Death does not know why this makes her stiffen.

'Thank you, Kitt.' Paedyn smiles at him. Another thing Death dislikes. 'You look very handsome.'

The king nods, offering an arm to his betrothed.

She accepts.

The doors begin to swing open.

'I see your ring made it back to the correct hand,' Kitt murmurs.

'Of course . . .'

Death has heard enough.

She doesn't care about their engagement. Truly. She is just bored.

Stepping out onto the balcony, Mara decides to descend the staircase to her left (it's an arbitrary choice to make). She then wades into the sea of sound and color that laps against the ballroom's ornate walls. Bodies sway around the room, glittering in the setting sunlight that streams through a dozen windows. An orange glow warms the sky beyond, ominous yet beautiful. Death quite likes that description. In fact, she finds herself standing before a window, watching the sky light up like a vibrant soul.

The king is now making a toast from the balcony above, but Death is far too occupied to notice. She weaves between each bejeweled being, beholding every bit of finery. But when the music resumes with an energetic melody, Mara takes her post against a pillar and observes the masses.

They drink and gossip and dance, their souls swirling before Death's eyes like splotches of colorful ink. The king is quickly tugged in every direction by a swarm of women before his betrothed drags him onto the dancefloor.

Mara looks away. There are more interesting things to witness — that, she is sure of.

She is quickly proven correct (per usual) when a flash of lilac hair draws her attention from across the ballroom. Even at this distance, Death can still make out a bickering Blair and Lenny. It is odd, though — not their constant quarreling, of course. For she had not expected the Tele to be released from her cage this evening.

And apparently, neither had the bride-to-be.

Paedyn lunges for Adena's killer in an impressive show of hatred. The gasping crowd closes in on the scene, obscuring Death's view of the entertainment she so craves. Though, mercifully, it seems that Mara does not miss much. The future queen is quick to stride from the scene she caused and guzzle a glass of champagne.

Death, beginning to enjoy herself now, flicks her gaze over the souls she has taken a liking to. Lenny seems relieved despite the look of loathing on his assignment's face. The Imperial then, assumedly, asks Blair to dance. Mara is quite certain that his offer is met with an array of condescension, but in the end, the unlikely pair is swaying.

Impossibly, their souls are slowly growing closer. Threads

of yellow and green begin to intertwine, burrowing into one another like barbs. And it hurts just as much, Death thinks, when two tied souls are torn apart.

'You're still here.'

The king steps beside the pillar, slipping his hands into the pockets of dark pants.

'I go where the entertainment is. And tonight, that is here,' Mara states.

Kitt's gaze traces the face of Death distantly. 'Is it boring, your . . . existence?'

Mara meets his stare. He likely wishes to keep his mind from the horrors he witnessed in the Mors. And Death, in an effort to disprove her monstrous reputation, indulges him. 'Why else would I take interest in the mundane lives of humans?'

The king finds this funny for some reason. He often unearths humor from the driest of Death's words. Perhaps her bluntness has been mistaken for humor.

They watch couples spin around the dancefloor.

Drunk and drunker.

Gingersnap and the bestower of such a title.

Paedyn and a stranger.

'Blair is here.' This is more of a declaration from Mara than it is a question.

Again, Kitt finds something about this comical. 'Have you been watching them?'

'As I said, entertainment.'

The king shakes his head. 'I'm trying to acclimate the two of them. Paedyn needs to get used to being around Blair, despite how difficult.'

'Hmm. And should you not be dancing with your betrothed?' Mara asks earnestly.

Kitt attempts a stiff shrug. 'It's not every day you get to talk to Death. I figured I would take advantage.'

Mara certainly does not find this flattering. Not even in the slightest. 'Is she part of your plan for this greater Ilya?'

A curt nod from the king.

'I see,' Death says, because she does.

This marriage has nothing to do with love.

'Strangely, I hope to see you again,' Kitt murmurs. He steps away from the pillar, retreating once again into his own mind. 'You're the only person I can talk to about dying.'

Mara watches him melt into the chaos before her.

She would see him again, Death decides.

He is entertainment. Nothing more.

Not nostalgia or meaning or a memory made man.

Besides, she has no soul left to tie to another. Not even to the shadow of her past.

'Can you believe she tried to attack me in front of the entire court?'

This is the third time Blair has reiterated her disbelief.

'Yes, actually, I can,' Lenny says, just as he has the last two times since slipping from the ballroom.

Death hears Blair trip over a stack of books behind her. It is quite dark in here, enough to have a human stumbling blindly. Not every creature feels so at home in the shadows.

The Tele's frustrated growl is smothered by Lenny's hushed warning. 'Keep your voice down. This is the last place you are supposed to be right now.'

'My voice is down,' she snaps. 'Everything is just loud when you have freakish hearing.' Blair takes three more steps before adding, 'This better be the right way, gingersnap.'

'I'm sorry,' he mumbles sarcastically. 'Would *you* like to lead us through this dark library with *your* Hyper vision? And—' he turns to see Blair glaring at a spot three feet to his right '—between the two of us, your hair color is way weirder than mine.'

Death ponders this. In fact, she thinks quite often on the unusual hair colors that pure power provided. But this Plague was picky — Death knows the feeling personally. Not all those in Ilya were fit for strength. And the silly humans never bothered to wonder why.

More books are plowed over by a huffing Blair. 'I can't see anything,' she says in a falsely sweet tone. 'I can't even tell if my loathing look is aimed at you.'

'Uh, turn your head to the left,' Lenny directs. 'Little more. Little – stop. Right there.'

'Just . . .' She makes a sound of disgust. 'Guide me.'

Death perches on a stack of books, watching Blair stick her hand into the darkness. She wears a look of utter annoyance. Mara finds her expressions inspirational.

Lenny shakes his head. Strides towards her. Slips his hand into hers.

He wears a look of concern Blair can't see. Mara wonders (as she often does) if this is due to a lack of repulsion at her touch. The thought is fleeting, though. Death is hardly the romantic she used to be.

The Imperial leads them between each towering bookcase, using that sharp vision of his to admire the intricate molding clinging to their corners. Mara follows dutifully. They weave through the massive library until a wall of books blocks their path.

'We are at the Elite records,' Lenny informs his peeved assignment. 'Also, why the hell are we at the Elite records?'

'Because I am not convinced you are using all your power,' Blair retorts dully. 'Now find the Hyper records.'

Yes, Death is very pleased she tagged along on this endeavor. Since the Imperial first sensed her presence in that hall, Mara has puzzled over how such a feat was possible. And this is her chance to discover the truth.

Lenny drags a finger across the worn spines. 'Not using all my power?' He scoffs. 'Look, I know you wanted to help make me stronger, or whatever, but I'm pretty sure I'd know how to use my ability.'

Death taps her foot against the worn floor.

Elites so love to pretend they understand the power they are given.

'Have you trained with it every day?' Blair interrogates. 'Pushed yourself to the point of exhaustion? Found your limits?'

The Imperial pulls a thin book from the shelf. 'Well, no, but—'

'Then you have no idea what you are capable of,' she cuts in dismissively. 'Your ability is like a muscle. If you want it to grow stronger you need to put in the work.'

'And out of the goodness of your heart,' Lenny says skeptically, 'you want to be my personal trainer?'

The Tele glares up at where she assumes Lenny's face to be (which happens to be his chin). 'You're hopeless, and I take pity on you.'

He shrugs. Sighs. 'Good enough for me.'

'Just read the book, gingersnap.'

Blair then yanks her hand free from his, as though she only just remembered it was being held.

Death has yet to determine her verdict on their souls. Perhaps they are not as hopeless as she had first thought. But Mara hates to be wrong, so she silently roots for their demise.

Begrudgingly, Lenny flips open the crumbling, leather cover. The pages are yellowed, each one dedicated to the Hyper ability. A century's worth of records rests beneath his fingers.

'Skip to the back,' Blair orders. 'There should be a section on the ability's development.'

'How do you know that?' the Imperial asks. 'I didn't think anyone opened these records.'

'The sergeant,' she huffs. 'She made me read the Tele volume when I was eight.'

'Right,' Lenny says slowly. His fingers fumble with a creased page. 'So, what about your dad? You don't talk about him much.'

Her mouth forms a mocking sound. 'There's not much to say. You wouldn't even believe he's the general when comparing him to my mother.' She tears shamelessly at the skin on her palm, forgetting that the Imperial can see the anxious habit. 'In his personal life, he's the one taking orders, not giving them. He just puts up with Mother better than I do.'

Lenny hums softly at her words. 'Sometimes it's better to stay with someone maddening than to go mad with loneliness.'

Surprisingly, this is met with no condescending remark. 'Maybe,' Blair finally mutters. She clears her throat. 'And your father?'

'Never met him,' Lenny answers distractedly. 'And from what I've heard, he's not worth missing.'

The sound of rustling pages fills the dark corner. Death leans over the Imperial's shoulder, noting that most of the book is blank. Flipping to the final entry, Lenny utters a dull, 'Wow. A Hyper's ability can develop a single sentence's worth.'

'Just read it,' Blair orders.

'Ahem.' The Imperial shakes his head before reciting the scrawled words. "In some cases, Hypers who learn to open their minds have developed a sixth sense."

Death has found her answer.

'Interesting,' Blair murmurs, voicing Mara's thoughts exactly.

'Interesting?' The Imperial blinks at the vague string of words. 'What the hell does that even mean?'

If only he could tap into that sixth sense now. Death would be happy to explain.

'Why are you asking me?' the Tele sneers. 'Open up your mind and find out.'

'And how does one go about doing that?'

'For starters, straighten your spine,' she snaps. 'I've never seen someone with such terrible posture. And, more obviously, don't stifle your power. Let it do as it pleases and see what happens.'

Lenny stares at her. 'How strangely encouraging of you.'

'I'm encouraging you not to be pathetic,' she clarifies with disgust.

'Well, me and my unstifled power can hear how fast your heart is beating.'

Scowling, Blair lifts her middle finger into the darkness.

'Saw that, too,' the Imperial says cheerily.

Yes, perhaps Death feels a bit guilty for preying on their downfall.

CHAPTER 15

Mara

Blair wakes with a jolt, gasping for air.

This manages to startle even Death from where she sits beneath a window (she can usually be found here, watching the sky display its colors – the Mors are obscenely dull in comparison).

Lenny is quick to peer down at the Tele, his freckled face drenched with concern. 'Are you all right?' He shakes his head. 'I think you were having a nightmare or something—'

Blair shoves him back with a surge of power. 'How long have you been awake?' she demands.

'Uh, a little while?' The Imperial blinks at her from across the room, looking impossibly more worried. 'You were sleeping, so I didn't want to bother you—'

'Well, you should have,' she seethes, sitting up in bed. 'I

don't need you watching over me.'

Mara stands to pace the perimeter of the room. She thinks better on her feet. Perhaps it is the rhythm her mind craves – something her still heart can no longer provide.

Hesitantly, Lenny asks, 'And why would that be a problem if I was?'

Death watches the Tele swallow thickly – perhaps her pride, because Blair finally murmurs, 'I dream about Adena. Often. And I don't want anyone to ever witness it.'

The Imperial lifts a brow. 'Witness what, exactly?'

'My weakness,' she bites out.

'Your—' Lenny laughs, drawing a scowl from Blair. 'Your weakness? You do know you're talking to a Hyper right now, yes?'

'I killed a criminal – or so I thought – and she haunts me every night!' the Tele blurts. 'Of course that makes me weak. And I'm supposed to be a general someday?' Now it is she who laughs, albeit humorlessly.

'You are not giving yourself enough credit,' Lenny scolds as he steps towards her. 'Don't worry. You are terrifying.'

'Maybe that is the problem,' the Tele ventures bitterly. 'Maybe I was meant to be like Adena. From what I've heard, she was passionate. Kind. Spirited.' Her voice grows oddly timid. Mara tilts her head at this shift in tone. 'What if that was who I could have been? A girl who dreamed and lived and pursued her passion. A girl who had two people willing to kill for her.'

'There is still time to be that girl, if you want,' Lenny says softly. 'Or you can remain exactly as you are – a frightening, frigid bitch. A compliment, of course,' he adds hurriedly. 'Look, you must feel cheated, like you never got a chance to figure out who you were – are. So do that now. We are killing you, after all. I doubt there will be a better time to start over.'

Sincerity coats his words, the type Mara knows a man only offers when he cares for someone. In return, Blair seems rather comforted by his receptive response. This alone has Death beginning to begrudgingly question how doomed these souls really are.

Lenny sits on the edge of the bed. To Mara's annoyance, the Tele allows this. 'But,' he starts slowly, 'you're allowed to be sharp, you know. Even the prettiest flowers have thorns.' His freckled face reddens. 'Not that I'm saying you're pretty – I mean, shit, you are pretty, but—'

'No need to embarrass yourself further,' Blair quips. 'I know I'm pretty. It's the only quality of mine people care to compliment.'

'Well, that's all you let them see.'

She forces her features into a dull expression. 'And you see something else?'

The Imperial shrugs. 'I see someone who became what they needed to. And that takes courage.'

They stare at each other. Too long.

'I want to find Paedyn.'

Blair's sudden demand startles her gingersnap. 'What? We aren't done forming the plan. Blair, this is a delicate matter—'

'There is nothing delicate about fake dying,' she snaps. 'I'm sick of waiting to begin my life. Just go get her and—'

'No.' Death didn't think Lenny was capable of such a stern objection. 'We have to do this right, or one of you may actually end up dead. We aren't ready.'

The Tele bristles at his blatant rejections. 'Fine.'

'Blair—'

'I'm hungry.' She gives him a mental shove off the bed. 'Will you at least get me food, or do you need time to plan your route to the kitchen?'

Lenny fights to find his footing beside the bed. 'Your condescension doesn't work on me.'

'I'll try harder next time.'

'I'm sure you will.' The Imperial fixes that white mask onto his face before striding towards the door. 'You know, you're annoyingly funny at my expense.' He steps into the hall. 'See, there is a compliment that has nothing to do with your appearance.'

Blair is quick to cover her slight smile with another demand. 'Tell Gail to add a dash of toasted coconut to her muffins. She can thank me later.'

'I'll be sure to relay your request in a less demeaning tone.'

Death takes her leave with the Imperial, stepping out into the hall where the floor falls away. There, atop the plush carpet, she sinks gracefully towards a different plane entirely. Her feet meet the cracked earth of her home, and it rumbles in approval at her arrival.

Yes, it is rather bleak here in the Mors, Death thinks as she takes in the brittle trees and wailing souls. But this is her eternity. Best not to compare her gloomy domain to the vibrance that the living so love to overlook.

With that in mind, Mara attends to the awaiting souls like any other day in the afterlife. She collects countless souls from everywhere life exists beyond the Mors. Some are rather peeved with Death (more than usual), because, admittedly, they have been trapped within their lifeless bodies for far too long. It can be quite claustrophobic, Mara imagines, being entombed in your own decaying flesh.

You see, a soul remains trapped within its vessel until Mara gathers and releases it into the Mors. Her time in Ilya, though strictly educational (or so she tells herself), has left Death a bit distracted. Souls have been neglected in their corpses for longer than Mara cares to admit, and she typically prides herself on efficiency.

After dragging a particularly grumpy spirit to its underwhelming afterlife, Death steps back onto the plane where sunsets are a normality, and heartbeats run rampant in every chest. She appears before Blair's door, only to find her standing outside it. Mara tilts her head at the scene she has stumbled upon.

A tall man stands opposite the Tele, his hair like a wave of midnight crashing over his brow. He is broad, his strong features only made less severe by the promise of dimples framing his mouth. And his gray eyes pin Blair to the wall.

'Just . . .' He points to her door. 'Get back in there. Please.'

Death knows this man. She walks a slow circle around his powerful body. Yes, he has delivered many souls to Mara. She has seen his stern face above the bodies he has drained of life. In fact, even she has heard whispers of this Elite.

Here stands the Enforcer of Ilya.

The brother to a dying king.

The Deliverer of Death, they say.

Mara would be the judge of that.

She halts before him, studying his soul. A flicker of surprise touches her features, witnessed by no one. A shimmering darkness swirls within him, sheer and threaded with strands of pure white.

Death blinks at such an odd sight. This is certainly not what she had expected.

'Hmm. It seems the Slummer taught you some manners. How ironic.'

There is that tiresome insult. Mara discerns, dolefully, precisely who it is the Tele refers to. For a woman with the gift of evading Death, she certainly deserves more respect from the living.

Blair's malice is like a reflex. It is as though she is wired to be his enemy, forced to forever find her worth in whether or not the Enforcer still considers her competition. The Tele had told the truth in that house (the one just beside those twisted trees uprooting the past) – she can't help but despise the Azer brothers.

The Enforcer's voice is low. 'Don't, Blair.'

Oh, but she does. And the Tele likely doesn't even know why.

'So will you share her with Kitt the rest of your life? Or find another Ordinary on the streets?'

Blair gasps sharply when the looming man slams her against the wall with a single thought. That has Death halting before him, her gaze searching his stern features. She is beginning to discover that this is no regular Elite, as they so enjoy calling themselves. No, his soul alone is a complexity that does not belong to Ilya.

The Enforcer steps towards Blair, who has found it futile to fight against her own power. The man is frighteningly calm, his threat little more than a murmur. 'Talk about her like that again, and you will be begging to stay locked in that room, safe from me.'

Mara believes him, for his soul calls to something within her.

'Shit.' The Tele lifts her widening gaze to his, nearly laughing. 'You're in love with her.'

Hmm. Another curious discovery.

Blair is abruptly released from the clutches of this man's mind. The Enforcer struggles to smother the shock on his face, and that is all the proof Death needs. Paedyn Gray's heart belongs to another – the brother of her betrothed.

'I always knew there was something between you, but . . .' This time, Blair does laugh. 'You're completely in love with her.'

The strongest Elite, brought to his knees by an Ordinary.

Ironic. Romantic. Doomed.

Mara has lived this tragedy.

The Tele steps forward slowly, still shaking her head at the lovesick prince. Her grin is cutting. 'Oh, you are fuc—'

'Prince Kai!'

Blair rolls her eyes at the familiar voice. The Imperial, rounding a corner, balances two plates of food while wearing a horrified expression beneath his mask. The glare he throws his assignment burns with betrayal. Lenny then clears his throat to make room for the wave of words about to flood from his mouth. 'Hello, sir, it's great to see you. Um, Blair, sweetheart, you're meant to be *in* the room. Not loitering outside of it, yes?'

'Um, Lenny,' the Tele starts sweetly, 'my little gingersnap that I could quite literally snap in half with a single thought, Kai spotted me before I had the chance to enter the room and send my sharpened knives flying towards those who pass beneath the window.' She addresses the Enforcer then. 'He loves that game. Don't let him tell you otherwise.'

(Death finally has a name for the infamous man using hers.) Death finds Lenny's immense discomfort rather entertaining. 'Quite the sense of humor she's got.' He herds the Tele towards her door. 'Never a dull moment with this one!'

'Oh, please,' she snaps. 'Don't pretend that you like me; it will only make me work harder to—'

The Imperial slams the door in her face.

'—ensure you don't,' Blair finishes furiously from within her room.

Mara remains in the hall, still immensely curious about this Deliverer of Death – of *her*. 'Keep her out of sight, all right?' he orders. 'It could have been Paedyn that walked down this hall, and we all know what she would have done.'

That was precisely what Blair was hoping for, Death wishes to shout at the humans. But there is no use. A lifetime ago, when Mara was young and still enthusiastic about her career, she would talk to the living. Not for them to hear, of course, but for her to never forget the voice of a gentle girl who died violently.

'Yes, sir.' Lenny nods in understanding. 'She can't stay locked up forever, though. It's not right.'

Mara is surprised by the Imperial's boldness on behalf of his assignment.

'I know.' The Enforcer sighs. 'But Paedyn needs time.' He turns then, setting a quick pace down the hall before calling over his shoulder. 'Good luck with her.'

'I don't need luck. She's not so bad,' Lenny murmurs.

The door swings open to display the patronizing pout on Blair's face. 'How sweet, gingersnap.'

'Shit!' He practically jumps at the sudden sight of her. 'What, did you have your ear to the door?'

'Like you couldn't hear me breathing,' she returns.

'Your intake of breath is the last thing I pay attention to.'

The Tele scowls. 'Then you are clearly still stifling your power.'

'No.' The Imperial's stern defiance is accompanied by a wagging finger in Blair's face. 'No, you don't get to do that. I'm the one who should be mad right now.'

'Go on, then,' she goads. 'Scold me. I could use a good laugh.'

Lenny steps into the room, his brows knit together. 'Fine. You can't sneak out like that again. What if the king throws me out before we even go through with the plan?'

Sneering, Blair steps close enough to have the Imperial swallowing. 'And what is that plan, exactly? It's time I light a fire under your ass, gingersnap. Otherwise, I'll never get out of here.'

The Imperial is hardly listening. No, his mind is somewhere else entirely.

'Fire,' he mutters.

A boyish grin spreads across his freckled face.

'I have an idea.'

Mara turns away from their hushed conversation to peer down the hallway.

The Enforcer is gone, and yet another mystery is unsolved.

But Death is unworried. They will meet again.

CHAPTER 16

Kitt

I sit on the fountain's edge, staring into the rippling water. Shillings lie motionless in their watery grave — another version of me had promised to distribute them to those in the slums.

I try not to think about Kai meeting the same fate. He insisted on accompanying my bride-to-be on her journey to Izram, and due to the aggravatingly sensible concerns he voiced, I was forced to watch him drift away on the *Reckoning*.

I lift my gaze to the sprawling gardens encircling me. They look dull in the setting sunlight, petals leeched of their vibrance. Weeks have passed since I last walked the spiraling paths through the grounds. Becoming king has hardly allowed me to enjoy myself as of late.

A sharp pang in my chest makes me flinch. My fingers curl into fists; eyes squeeze shut.

'You are worse than you were after dying.'

I blow out a breath before meeting Death's gaze. She stands a few feet to my left, her hands tucked into the deep pockets of her cloak. The gaping hood swallows her auburn hair, shades the placid features beneath.

'The Plague hasn't been kind to me,' I admit distantly.

'That's because it wasn't meant for you.'

I can hardly find the strength to chuckle. 'Should I even bother asking you to elaborate? Or is Death required to be this cryptic?'

'You will find out soon enough,' Mara answers evenly. 'But you have already learned more about the afterlife than most.'

'I'm not sure I have.' I stand with a sigh. 'It's been days since I . . . died, and I'm not entirely sure what even happened.'

Death's gaze dips for a single moment. 'Walk with me? I will answer your questions about the Mors.'

Mara's offer and the hesitancy that accompanies it makes me pause. 'Yes, of course.' I stride towards her. 'That sounds like a fair deal.'

Her cloak drags along the stone path, swallowing stray petals and muffling the sound of each step. We embrace the silence that wedges its way between us. I haven't felt comfortable being anything but a king as of late, so I relish in the simplicity of this moment. Who knew a stroll with Death could bring such peace.

'I haven't seen you in a few days,' I finally say, brushing my fingers along a row of reaching flowers.

Mara answers quickly. 'Have you been looking for me?'

'Well, I didn't think it was a good sign, me seeing you.' I say this with a touch of humor, but if Death ever does smile, that certainly doesn't coax one from her lips.

'Of course,' she agrees softly. 'My presence is never wanted.'

There is no evidence of hurt in her voice, and still, I feel a twinge of guilt in my gut. I'm not sure why I wish to lift Death's spirits – I'm not entirely sure she even has them. 'Truth be told, I might have been looking for you,' I say, and it might just be the truth. 'Like I said at the ball, it's nice, having someone to talk to about . . . everything.'

She finally looks at me then, brown eyes on the verge of portraying an emotion. 'I know what it feels like to be alone. That is why I wanted to meet you.'

I nod at the pink sky hanging low over us. 'And it is only me you can talk to?'

'My connection with your dying soul allows me to physically interact with you while remaining unnoticed to others. Think of it like a veil.' Mara slips her hand from a pocket to lift a drooping flower. It's an odd sight from Death. 'I can only step onto this plane through the sliver of opening you've offered me. But to everyone else, I remain a shadow.'

'So—' our shoulders brush as we follow the curving path '—where do you go when you're not with me?'

'I have other souls to take care of.' It almost sounds like she's teasing me. 'The dead await their afterlife.'

I cough into a fist, ignoring Mara's scrutiny. She's more watchful than the Healers. 'The Mors seemed . . . horribly lonely. The afterlife is hardly anything to look forward to.'

'You didn't enjoy it,' she observes.

I glance over at her. 'Why would I?'

'I just thought I understood you better.' She holds my gaze. 'You have a darkness within you. One I figured would be drawn to the Mors.'

'There is no darkness within me.'

The words tear off my tongue, bitter and biting. I blink in surprise at my sudden irritation. 'Sorry,' I murmur earnestly. 'I'm not sure what came over me.'

'Hmm.' That soft sound of fascination is all she offers in response.

I look away. Draw in a deep breath.

Hmm, indeed.

Sunlight flees from the sky as we tread between rows of tangled foliage. Mara looks as completely unreadable as always, irritatingly elusive. Everything about Death is uncertain, down to the very moment she snatches your soul.

I clear my throat. 'So, I never found my mother.'

'I'm sorry.'

The words are genuine. What a strange sentence coming from Death's mouth.

'It's frustrating, but my temporary death wasn't in vain.' I steer us back towards the towering fountain. 'I found my father.'

'Edric Azer,' Mara reminisces. 'An angry soul.'

'Even more so after what I told him.'

The look on Father's face, the color draining from it, is a fond memory I frequently relive. Mere weeks ago, I would have never dreamed of speaking to him like that. He was everything to me, and I was determined to be *something* to him.

But I was a boy then. Now I am a king.

Mara's gaze pierces me from beneath her yawning hood. 'And what did you say?'

'The truth.' I clear my tightening throat with a cough. 'I am going to be so much greater than him. *He* was too weak to do what needs to be done – not me.' Agitation returns to my voice. 'And he will spend the rest of his afterlife thinking about that. Thinking about the disappointing son who will bury his legacy.'

'I'm sure he will,' she says simply. Mara doesn't seem disturbed by my blatant desire for vengeance. 'Souls like his don't usually find peace.'

We slow to a stop before the fountain. 'Find peace?'

'Those who accept that there is no way out of the Mors are the ones who escape it.' Death says this like one would when solving an obvious riddle. 'They move on. Dwell within the very fabric of the Mors. Each soul may decide how they spend their afterlife – forever searching for a way to escape it or greeting fate and finding peace.'

I stare at her in disbelief. 'So, the afterlife is all just one big mind game?'

'It's not fire or paradise.' She almost shrugs. 'It's what you make of it. But Death is consistently lonely.'

I vaguely wonder if she is speaking about herself when a ripple of realization has me murmuring, 'My father . . . He was convinced Iris was whispering to him from inside a tree.'

'She likely was.' The words actually sound sane when Mara says them so dully. 'The trees are quite talkative.'

'So, there is no way to reach my mother?' I can't help but feel disappointed, despite how selfish. 'Because she found peace?'

'Her soul is resting.' The sadness in Mara's voice is startling. No emotion has ever been so evident. 'That is all anyone can hope for.'

'Is that what you hope for?' I ask boldly.

'I am not allowed to hope. Not since before.' There is that pinch of sadness again. 'And I hardly remember that lifetime.'

I utter the same set of words I had when the sun still lit the sky. 'Should I even bother asking you to elaborate?'

She says nothing.

'How long have you been Death?'

A tedious, still moment passes. I think this, too, is a futile use of my breath until—

Her gaze grows distant. 'Long enough to forget how to live.'

This answer only brings on another onslaught of questions that I'm forced to swallow.

Who is — was — Mara?

The more I know about her, the less I understand.

Human.

She was a living, breathing being at some point.

Death is ageless. Mara is not.

So how did she end up dragging souls to the Mors?

I look down at my reflection in the fountain's crisp pool. My confusion is reflected there, rippling beneath me to deepen the creases in my brow. The only thing I'm certain of is Death's longing to live, and my impending doom.

Sighing, I look up at the mystery that is Mara. 'I'm dying, aren't I? Like truly, undeniably not going to survive this Plague?'

A shadow of sympathy crosses her face. 'Your body wasn't meant to handle such power. I'm not sure how much time you have . . .'

'Right.'

I nod, again and again. As if that is all it takes for me to accept the consequences of what I've done for power. 'Tell you what,' I start with a sigh. 'I'll remind you how to live if you teach me how to die.'

At first, Mara says nothing. Then, she offers a soft 'Hmm.'

I shake my head. 'You're either in or you're out, Death. And neither of us really have anything to lose.'

'Fine,' she says, and by the sound of it, against her better judgment. 'I'm in.'

I stretch my power towards the pool of water below. Since becoming king, my Dual ability is hardly needed within the confines of my study. In fact, over the past few weeks, I've done little more than light the occasional candle or drench a parched plant. But when I order the fountain's water to lift and nuzzle my hand, it hesitates. My power feels somehow distant, unfamiliar in my veins.

I frown, concentrating in a way I haven't had to since I was a boy.

The Plague.

Water rushes towards me suddenly, propelling a dull coin to the surface. I smile slightly, relieved by my responding power. Mara watches closely as the stream of water places a shilling into my palm. It's still dripping as I hold it between us. 'All right, let's flip a coin for who has the first lesson.'

Death dips her chin in agreement.

'Heads, you teach me how to die first.' I explain. 'Tails, we start with living.'

Silver glints in the dim light as I flip the shilling.

When it returns to my palm, Mara leans in to see the verdict.

'Tails.' I smile. 'Time to remind you how to live.'

After a moment of concentration, I send a wave of water

crashing into Death. It's perhaps not the wisest choice.

And, terrifyingly, she doesn't even flinch.

Her wet hood droops around the blank expression she still wears. Beads of water drip from her cloak, down her nose, as she utters, 'What . . . was that?'

If it weren't for the faintest hint of amusement on her face, I fear I might have dropped dead. 'This is your first lesson on living – surprises.'

'Hmm.'

I don't have time to react before water is thoroughly drenching me.

Looking up through dripping lashes, I sputter at Mara. Shockingly, her lips curl ever so slightly at the corners. I feel a bit honored to be bestowed with such muted expression. 'Surprise,' she says evenly. 'I can do that too.'

I blink at her.

Then I laugh. For the first time in weeks, *I laugh.*

'To living with you, Mara.'

I lift the coin between us.

She drips before me, gaze unwavering.

'To accompanying you in death, Kitt.'

CHAPTER 17

Mara

The king's bed is quite soft.

Death sits on its edge, of course, not tucked beneath the covers beside a dozing Kitt. Though, she does wish to remember what that feels like—a strong arm tugging her close, warm breath tickling her neck. But perhaps all Azers feel the same. Perhaps she has already loved and loathed this king a lifetime before. Perhaps there is no need to do so again.

(Or perhaps this time could be different.)

Mara watches a crease form between the king's brows, moonlight pooling in that splinter of tension marring his skin. She is frequently fascinated by sleep, for it is the art of balancing Life and Death (you see, they don't often enjoy each other's company). Such blissful stillness allows one to hide

within a state of pure existence. And Mara envies such limbo, such nothingness at all.

Kitt wakes with a jolt, shoving covers from his sticky skin. Those green eyes (the ones that recklessly wandered in a past life) find Death's in the darkness, and he startles again at the sight of her. It is understandable, really, such a reaction to her perched on one's bed. Mara does not have a good reputation for leaving souls alive once she has visited them in the night.

'M–Mara?'

The king sounds surprised, but not afraid. Never afraid of her.

(And Death likes that very much.)

'You were having a nightmare,' Mara informs, as though he is unaware. 'Your distress summoned me.'

(This is partially true. Death had already made herself comfortable at his bedside before his unease called to her, but that is neither here nor there.)

Kitt nods groggily. 'I'm sorry.'

'Sorry?' Mara tilts her head, a habit that refused to die when she did. 'What for?'

'It must be . . .' The king scours his muddled mind before shrugging sluggishly. 'It must be annoying. You know, constantly being summoned but not seen.' He blinks blearily at her through the shadows. 'You're forced to feel everything, but never for yourself.'

The words are uttered with such sincerity, such innocence

in the face of iniquity, that Death fears her cold heart might beg to beat once again. For it wishes to recall the simplicity of assuming goodness in everyone, everything. But this is a luxury for the living alone. Naivety—a blessing and a curse—is precisely what had Mara stumbling into Death so long ago. Now Kitt has done the same.

So human, this man before Mara. He sits within the coiled sheets, awaiting a docile answer from an unassumingly savage creature. Death watches him (always, but especially now) look at her like a misunderstanding, like more than a monster of the Mors. And she quite likes to be thought of as such—a girl deserving of a boy's attention, because he wishes to give it to her, not because he fears what will happen otherwise.

'I would not wish this afterlife on my worst enemy,' Mara finally offers the king. For his kindness, his bizarre understanding of her, has something swelling in Death's chest. She promptly ignores it, of course. For his sake.

Kitt nods. His gaze is heavy on the face of Death.

(Regrettably, she likes that as well.)

They sit among the shadows, content to bask within their shared stillness. Mara, you see, is now old enough to appreciate peaceful solidarity. There was once a time—when she was young and, well, quite alive—when such silence was cynical. But now she relishes the comfort of simply existing alongside another.

'What were you dreaming about?' Death finally asks after retreating from her thoughts.

The king's heavy sigh is followed by a sharp cough. 'My deepest fear becoming reality.'

'And what is that?'

There is no hiding from Death. The king knows this, and that is why he answers. 'Becoming a monster.'

Mara considers this. 'You fear your plans for Ilya and the kingdoms will make others believe you to be a monster?'

There is a beat of silence before a choked 'yes' forms on Kitt's lips.

'You worry what Kai will think of you,' Death observes plainly, as she always does. 'So why go through with it all?'

The king hangs his head, hair still ruffled with the remnants of sleep. 'I want to be greater than my father, yes. But more than that, I . . . I don't want anyone to feel the way I did, the way I *have*, my whole life.' His eyes lift then, wild with sudden determination, to meet Mara's gaze. 'If I do this— make us all Elites, even the playing field—then there will be nothing else to live up to. No son or daughter will ever be disregarded, used. Because as long as there are Ordinaries and Elites'—Kitt breathes—'there will always be divide, always some hard, terrible decision to make. But I won't let anyone else be raised to simply carry out some legacy.' He laughs, the sound quivering with emotion. 'No, I'll do that for them. I'm finishing this for good.'

Death studies this resolute royal. 'You really have thought this through.'

'I know people think I'm mad,' Kitt admits. 'And if they don't already, then they certainly will.' He swallows thickly. 'But before I was a king, I was a boy who begged to be loved by one. All because my father was too focused on the power Ordinaries lacked. And look at how I turned out—broken.' Another trembling laugh. 'We don't need any more Kitts in this kingdom. No, I will be the beginning of something better. Something whole.'

That comfortable silence returns.

The moon leans in through the window, peering down at Death and her willing victim. They wait for whatever words follow, expectant but not entirely hurried. Rather, it is quite nice to linger, together, between this moment and the next.

'You will not reap the benefits of this new world,' Mara eventually reminds him, ever the pessimist.

'But Kai will.' The king drags an ink-stained hand over his drawn face. 'For once, I will do the dirty work for him. In the end, this future will be far kinder than his past.'

'That's admirable.' This does not mean much coming from Death, but she says it nonetheless.

Kitt looks startlingly hopeful at her words. 'You don't think I'm a monster?'

'I don't think you know what a monster is yet.'

'Maybe not.' He then inches closer to Death (in more ways than one), his eyes flicking over her. 'Because you certainly don't look like one.'

'What is it I look like?'

'A trap.' Kitt smiles—genuine and boyish. The way only an Azer knows how. 'But I don't think that is what you are. Not really.'

Death's voice is steady despite her anticipation. 'Go on.'

'I think you are a beautiful being forced to do ugly things.' The king looks suddenly serious. 'You're not malicious—no. You're obedient.'

Mara, if she had any blood pumping through her veins, might have blushed. But her voice, predictably, remains dull. 'So, what do you think? Am *I* a monster?'

'I'm not afraid of you.'

'That is not what I asked.'

Green eyes behold Death, more gently than she deserves. 'You don't look like him. So no, I do not think you are a monster.'

But Kitt does not stop there. If he had, perhaps things would have been different. But if you give Death hope, she will surely kill you with it.

'In fact,' he says slowly, 'I would have believed you were a deity, if only you said so. I wouldn't have questioned worshiping something so divine.'

CHAPTER 18

Mara

'Plagues, you have to be the worst Hyper in Ilya.' The Imperial cannot currently see the lazy disapproval on Blair's face with a scarf tied over his eyes, but Death witnesses it clearly from where she sits atop the bed.

'Well, I am but a lowly Mundane,' Lenny mutters dully. 'I'm not sure what you expected from this exercise—'

'I expected,' she growls, 'an Elite to actually *use* their power. Now open up your senses.'

The Imperial shifts uncomfortably on the wood floor. 'This is a waste of time.'

'Any time with you could be better spent,' the Tele sneers impressively. 'Now smell.'

She uncorks a vial. Mara scans the remarkable assortment of spices in Blair's collection as she orders, 'Describe the notes.'

'It's hard to smell anything past the scarf wrapped around my head,' Lenny mumbles.

This has Blair scowling. 'It doesn't smell like anything.'

'It smells like you.'

The Tele blinks. Death is fortunate enough to have a front-row seat as Blair grapples for composure. After straightening her spine and picking at that skin on her left palm, she finally commands, 'Then smell harder.'

Lenny sighs in exasperation, unaware how his knowledge of the Tele's scent has affected her. 'Uh . . .' Even while sitting several feet away, he is able to pull apart each layer of the faint aroma Blair has unleashed. 'It's spicy, but there is a hint of sweetness.'

'Do better.'

'Fine, uh, I'm getting a hint of citrus at the top,' the Imperial ventures. 'Then something earthier, like . . .' He seems to be pushing his power, chasing after that final undertone. 'Like wood. Pine.'

Blair actually sounds pleased. 'Not bad. It would be a shame if you couldn't identify the spice that shares your name.'

Frowning, Lenny pulls the scarf from his face. 'What was it?'

The sun has long set since they began this odd training (hence why Mara isn't perched beneath her window), but Death can clearly see Blair's smug expression as she lifts the vial. 'Ginger, obviously.'

'Ha ha.' He shakes his head in defeat. 'You know what, calling me by my real name is just as offensive. I'm cursed to be a "Lenny," and Ma still has the audacity to say she loves me.'

Mara tilts her head at the frigid smile that touches a corner of Blair's lips. 'I'm sure it's nice to hear, nonetheless.'

Her words seem to sober the Imperial. Not everyone is on the receiving end of such affection. And those who are, Death thinks bitterly, will only end up hurt.

'It is nice,' Lenny says softly.

It looks as though he is about to stumble through some sort of sincerity when Blair returns to her formalities. 'Those are all the spices I have with me,' she informs, gesturing to the hidden chest she retrieved from beneath a floorboard. Vials are scattered atop the wood beside her crossed legs. 'But tomorrow, you will ask Gail for a dozen more so we can test your smell again. It is your weakest link, and that is saying a lot.'

Lenny ignores the pointed dig to nod instead at the only spice left within the box. 'What about that one?'

The Tele's gaze darts to the confined brown powder. 'We aren't using that one. It's nutmeg.'

Mara leans in, her interest piqued.

Lenny mirrors Death with a slight smile tugging at his lips. 'Do you not like nutmeg or something?'

'Why would I like nutmeg?' she snaps. 'Nutmeg is insufferable. And I hate it.'

Death has the strangest feeling that the Tele is no longer

speaking about a spice. In fact, if she were to study the exact shade of Lenny's eyes, Mara might just compare it to a rich sprinkling of nutmeg. But that is just her opinion, of course. Perhaps Blair is thinking nothing of the sort. (Though, Death is rarely wrong about these things.)

'Whoa.' Lenny lifts his palms into the air where she can see them. 'Yeah, sure, nutmeg is the worst.'

This seems to satisfy Blair's sudden surge of anger. With a sigh, she begins placing each vial back into its designated spot within the chest. 'You're improving. It's good to know you aren't a complete lost cause.'

The Imperial harrumphs halfheartedly. It has been a week since the future queen set sail for Izram (a kingdom Death frequents in her gathering of souls, though she does not have to brave the Shallows to do so), and they have spent every day since then pushing the Imperial's power to its fullest.

Mara watches Blair (as does Lenny, both intensely and quite often) hide a piece of her passion beneath that floorboard, stifling the box of spices. And with every passing day, that skin on her palm only grows more mangled.

The Imperial clears his throat. 'Why are you helping me again?'

'Don't ask, or I might change my mind,' she retorts. 'Besides, your idea to incorporate fire into my death was surprisingly not stupid.'

(Death is looking forward to such impending disaster.)

'Thanks?'

'Don't thank me,' the Tele snaps. 'I am simply repaying a debt.'

'Right,' Lenny agrees sarcastically. 'Not an ounce of goodness in your heart, huh?'

Blair's gaze is now sternly set on his. 'I'm not sure what is in my heart. It's likely hollow.'

Mara considers this. Her heart no longer beats at all, so she feels unfit to form a proper opinion. This rarely happens, seeing that drawing correct conclusions is her favorite pastime.

The Imperial's consideration is followed by a lazy shrug. 'All the more space to hold the things you love.'

Blair struggles not to gape at his words. Something suspiciously close to awe falls over her features before it is quickly smothered with indifference. 'That was unsurprisingly stupid.'

At this point in the night, Death kindly leaves them to their boredom. She strides out into the hall with a foreign feeling of excitement tangling in her stomach. Yes, Mara is looking forward to learning how to live this evening. But her veiled zeal has nothing to do with the king's company, of course.

He is waiting for her in the kitchen with a towel slung over his shoulder. Kitt's hair is a disheveled collection of golden strands that displays his frustration in the path his fingers have continually combed. His green gaze meets Mara in the doorway, warming at the sight of her.

That rarely happens when one lays eyes on Death. Quite the opposite tends to occur, actually. For this reason, she can hardly help the shadow of a smile that creeps across her stiff features.

'Are you ready for your lesson on living?' he says by way of greeting.

In truth, Mara has been waiting all week since their conversation in the gardens. But the king is understandably busy, what with running a kingdom and slowly dying, so Death graciously gave him some space. Or so he thinks. She has, of course, observed him from afar since the very beginning. His meetings with the Scholars, nonsense with the Healers, and most interestingly, his dinners with Paedyn Gray.

None of this matters, Death reassures herself. It cannot.

This may come as a shock, considering how levelheaded and stoic Mara is, but she has been known to become rather obsessive.

But that is not this.

Entertainment, remember?

'I am ready,' Mara answers honestly. She strides into the kitchen, taking her place beside him. 'What will I be learning?'

Kitt grins as he pulls a bag of flour from the cupboard clinging to the wall above. His hands are stained with ink. 'Creation – in its simplest form, obviously. I thought we could attempt to bake something.'

Slightly ironic, considering the Tele that had been exclusively trapped in her room until Paedyn's departure, but Death is not opposed to the idea. 'Attempt?'

'If we manage to make something edible—' the king shakes his head '—I'll consider this a success.'

Mara watches as Kitt gathers an assortment of ingredients. He sets them on the counter, never slowing for a single second. Death notes the dark circles beneath his eyes, the stretching of his skin atop sharp cheekbones. Yes, his blue soul is dimming with every passing day.

'Do the Healers still have you taking their useless herbs?' Mara asks evenly.

Kitt glances over at her. 'They do. But I like to think they help a little bit.'

At the king's direction, Mara dumps flour into a bowl. 'They don't. Healers no longer know how to heal without their borrowed power.'

'How do you know so much about Ilya?' Kitt asks skeptically.

'How do you know so little about your own kingdom?'

It's as though he cannot help but chuckle. 'You speak your mind. I appreciate that.'

'Death does not have time to waste.'

'No, I'm sure you don't,' he returns. 'It's still so strange that you are here. A physical being.'

Mara stands idly beside the king as he cracks an egg into the bowl, adding several shells to the other ingredients. She really is not much help. 'We can be honest with each other, Kitt,' she says evenly, the use of his name somehow intoxicating. 'What surprises you the most is Death being a woman.'

'Maybe at first.' His tired eyes meet Mara's. 'Only because I expected such brutality from a man.'

'I am not a killer.' Her correction is clipped.

A crease forms between the king's brows. 'But you are . . . Death.'

'I am the absence of Life,' Mara says simply. 'Just as darkness is merely a lack of light. I only collect souls when Life decides to let them go.'

Kitt stops his struggled stirring to stare at her. 'So, you're saying it is Life that kills?'

'It is Life that gives up, not Death that takes away. Though, it is my reputation that suffers.' Mara drags her finger through a dusting of flour atop the counter. 'No matter. Humans need someone to blame. I don't mind being their villain.'

The king shakes his head. 'I'm sorry. That doesn't seem fair.'

There this king goes again, understanding Death.

'It is not fair,' she agrees simply. 'But I'm quite good at retribution, if I so desire.' A heartbeat later (Kitt's, of course), and Death is already moving on from the morbid topic. 'So, what is it we are attempting to bake?'

'Right.' The king runs a hand through his hair, raking fingers through that paved path. 'Yes, I'm supposed to be reminding you how to live. You'll have to wait your turn to further educate me on dying.' He forces a smile onto his features. Mara quite enjoys the warmth he exudes, though opposite from her in every way. 'Now, I was hoping to make a batch of Ilya's favorite treat—'

'Sticky buns,' Death finishes. 'I've heard.'

His brows lifts. 'Have you ever had one?'

'I don't eat.'

The king's face falls. 'Oh. *Oh.* I really did not think this through, did I?' He chuckles uncomfortably. 'My mind has been a bit jumbled lately—'

'But I can,' Mara cuts in. She does not want to disappoint him. And she certainly does not ponder why that is.

'Oh, good.' Kitt sighs in relief. 'Well, then, you will need one of these.' He lifts an apron from a nearby hook. 'You might want to take off your cloak.'

Death, who has never done such a thing in all her years as a resident of the Mors, unclasps the thick wool from around her shoulders to reveal a fitted ensemble of black beneath. Stepping closer, the king takes her weathered cloak, hangs it on the free hook, and looks down at a watchful Mara. He then loops the apron's strap around Death's neck to crown her with the stained fabric. If she had any breath to hold, she might have done just that when he reaches around her waist (his arms brush her hips, which Mara barely notices, of course) to tie a knot behind her back.

'There,' he murmurs, rather close to her ear. 'Now you

shouldn't get covered in flour. No promises, though.'

Death watches him return to the counter. She then finds her composure and follows.

Kitt tips the bowl over, shaking it slightly to free the thick dough from within. It plops onto the counter, its consistency less than promising. The king and his shadow of Death stare at what they have made.

'Is it supposed to look like that?' Mara asks earnestly.

Kitt almost laughs. 'I have no idea.'

He attempts to knead the dough into something more appealing. But it is lumpy and dry and peppered with eggshells. Finally, the king steps back to stare at the mutilated creation.

'You know what . . .' He shakes his head. 'Living is a mess. It's complicated and chaotic most of the time. So—' he reaches around Mara once again, tugging the laces there free with a single pull '—forget the apron. This is all the lesson on life you need.'

Death slips out of the thin cloth. 'I don't understand.'

Smiling, Kitt dips a hand into the bag of flour. Then a powdered finger is dragging down Mara's nose. 'What do you feel?' he asks, his eyes brighter than they have been in days.

Death blinks at the grinning king. 'I feel flour on my nose.'

Now both of Kitt's palms are completely white. He cups Mara's face with them. 'And now?'

She stares up at him. No one can touch Death like this, and

if they could, they certainly wouldn't dare. She had forgotten what it felt like to be held. And in this moment, Mara is suddenly afraid of what she would do to feel this way again. 'I feel . . . an exhilarating lack of control,' Death realizes.

The king's smile only widens.

His gritty hands are still on Mara's face.

Yes, Death made a grave mistake coming here.

'*That*,' he breathes, 'that is what it feels like to live.'

Mara remembers now. She remembers this feeling. It was once associated with a ghost.

The sound of approaching footsteps has Kitt pulling away. Another feeling Death knows all too well.

'Blair, don't—'

The warning whisper is lost within the sound of squealing door hinges. The unbothered Tele strides into the kitchen, her boots sinking into the puddle of light.

'Oh,' she says dully. 'It's you.'

This is addressed to Kitt, of course, though Mara stands unseen beside him, covered in flour.

Lenny skids to a stop behind his assignment. Then swallows at the sight of his king. 'Your Majesty. I apologize for the intrusion.'

And Death thought this night couldn't get any more interesting.

'Blair.' Kitt clears his throat. He fights to keep his gaze from straying towards Mara. 'This is the last place I expected to find you.'

Her gaze flicks to the poor excuse for dough. 'The feeling is mutual.'

The Imperial clears his throat. 'Your Majesty, I figured since Paedyn is off on her second Trial, Blair could stretch her legs a bit. But we will leave you to your—' he too glances at the creation atop the counter '—baking.'

'No, it's fine.' The king drags floured palms down his tunic. 'We— I am done for the night.'

His gaze shifts to Death, unbidden. She nods.

Yes, it is rather nice to be noticed.

Lenny's gaze drifts around what he believes to be an empty room. 'Uh, thank you, Your Majesty.'

'Enjoy your free time, Blair,' Kitt offers, making his way to the door. 'But if Paedyn makes it back, you will have to return to your room for a little while longer.'

The Imperial stiffens slightly at the king's lack of confidence in his betrothed. Mara, who cannot help but wonder, thinks that perhaps Kitt does not intend for Paedyn to return. This is hardly an unreasonable accusation, considering the deadly incident that drew Death to her side.

She was suspended in the air above a raging sea. Mara now finds these situations Paedyn Gray gets herself into unsurprising. But she watched from afar, waiting to see if her services were actually needed. Of course, they were not. The Enforcer pulled her back aboard the ship, evading yet another run-in with Death herself.

Yes, Mara would have to inquire about this.

'You haven't hydrated your flour,' Blair points out with more than a little contempt. 'That is why your dough looks like shit.'

Lenny winces at her words. But the king only gives her a look that speaks to their rocky relationship. 'I'll keep that in mind for next time.'

'You do that,' the Tele calls after him.

Kitt strides from the kitchen as Death plucks her cloak from the hook, slinging it over floury shoulders before following.

Blair's ire grows distant behind the closing doors. 'What a waste of perfectly good ingredients. I'll salvage it. Now, listen closely, gingersnap – you of all people should be able to do that. I need a lemon, warm water, cinnamon sticks . . .'

The king rounds a corner, shaking his head. 'I see why you watch them.'

Mara stares longingly down the hall.

'You want to go watch them now, don't you?' Kitt sighs.

'Something is happening between their souls,' Death says. 'I thought they were doomed, but now I'm not so sure.'

The king shakes his head. 'Their souls?'

'Something you will learn when I teach you how to die.'

'Deal.' Kitt smiles sadly then. 'And . . . thank you. It's easy to feel like myself when I'm with you.'

Mara does not tell him that the feeling is likely due to his soul drifting towards her – towards Death. He feels better in her presence due to this morbid connection drawing them together. Nothing more.

(But maybe, just maybe, something more.)

'Good night,' this Azer says softly. He looks like so many before him. Kitt turns to leave before glancing over a shoulder. 'That night in the hall . . . You were serious about not sleeping, weren't you?'

'Deathly so,' Mara says evenly. 'I'm afraid I always am.'

He nods, his slight smile warming something within Death's cold chest. 'I'm beginning to learn that. Oh, and—' he gestures vaguely to Mara's complexion '—you have a little something on your face.'

She might have let a small smile slip onto her stoic features. 'It's a good thing only you can see me.'

'Yes.' Kitt turns away. 'I have Death all to myself.'

The king does indeed.

And if he weren't already doomed to die, Death's newfound infatuation would certainly be fatal.

CHAPTER 19

Mara

Death often thinks on the fragility of Life.

Not humans themselves, per se, but how carelessly they are handled by a fickle fate. One wrong move, one lapse in judgment, and the living are discarded for Death to catch. You see, Life does not tolerate that which makes her look weak. For this reason, so few (it seems) remain in her good graces.

Mara ponders this as she watches a dying king attempt to keep up with his powerful brother. They spar in a dirt ring, swords glinting in the shy streams of morning sunlight. Their smiles and breathless laughter speak to the bond buried deep between them.

How boyish they seem. Death has been watching them for only a short time, but that is what she concludes. Along with how unfair her present occupation is. Mara takes no satisfaction

in ripping these souls apart. But Life has given up on Kitt Azer, leaving her to blame for his demise.

She usually does not mind looking like the bad guy, taking the fall for Life's impulsive decisions. But not with him. No, for some terrible reason, Death wants him to think of her fondly.

The clashing of steel summons Mara's attention once more, where she finds the royals caught in a sharp embrace, their blades crossed closely between them. Here, the Enforcer has a moment to study his brother's drawn face. 'Are . . . are you all right?'

Death tilts her head at his astute observation.

The king shoves away from his brother. 'Why do you ask?'

Kitt knows precisely why his brother asks. He looks worse than Death. In fact, most find Death to look quite enticing.

Kai shakes his head. 'Something . . . feels different.'

Curious, this prince.

'I've been a bit under the weather recently.' Kitt's lies are casually strung together. 'It will pass, I'm sure.'

It will not.

'Now,' he pants, 'have you been out here all night?'

The brother lets out a labored laugh. 'After all these years, that shouldn't surprise you.'

Kitt is entirely too enthralled to notice Death's presence. Or, perhaps he has simply grown used to her watchful gaze. She much prefers that theory. Familiarity is intimate.

'I figured you were with Paedyn,' the king says far too casually.

Several blows later, Kai manages, 'I haven't . . . I haven't seen her since the cellar.'

Ah, yes. The cellar.

Pacing around that table, filled to the brim with food and a chattering court, Mara had observed the extravagant feast in honor of Paedyn's return from her second Trial. A sham, to be certain, as the king once told her the Ordinary was simply a pawn in his great, albeit flawed, plan for Ilya.

Still, Death enjoyed herself. She listened to Lenny's distress over how many forks were set before him while Blair offered her condescension rather than comfort. Mara then relished the way Kitt's eyes continually found hers from across the room, or the way his lips twitched when she whispered her findings about his court.

One man was wearing two different colored socks. Another was on his fourth plate of food. The woman beside her was commenting on Paedyn's hair and how, for an Ordinary, it actually looked quite nice.

Death, and the soul that would soon be hers, carried on like this until the king was obligated to make a toast. His bride-to-be followed suit, though hers was little more than a threat thrown at Blair. The tension was then alleviated by the dismissal of this entertaining dining experience when the trio (plus Death) made their way to the cellar below.

There, Mara watched Kitt's worries melt away when he

lovingly referred to his brother as 'Kai Pie'. Paedyn and the brothers she had unknowingly tugged apart spent most of the night swallowing wine when their mouths weren't bubbling with laughter.

But it was Kai the king focused his attention on. This, more than the Enforcer's want for a betrothed woman, was obvious. Now, with the prince's safe return to Ilya, Kitt wastes no time in his brother's presence. For he has little left.

'I'm surprised,' the panting king says in the center of that dirt ring. This, of course, is in response to Kai's supposed lack of contact with the future queen.

Kai blocks a swift blow. 'And why would that surprise you?'

'You know why.'

'Enlighten me,' the Enforcer dares.

Death leans on a weapon rack, her anticipation growing.

'Because you love her!' the king blurts raggedly. He lowers his sword, defeated. 'Perhaps more than anything.'

Mara is growing rather good at recognizing fear within Kitt, ever since learning of the nightmare that plagues him. But the fear she now senses is nagging, stalking the king in broad daylight. Unlike most, it is not her – Death. But rather, the lack of love from the one person who has seen all of him.

Kai swallows. 'Don't be ridiculous, Kitty. She is your bride.'

'And I am your brother,' the king returns. 'Always. No matter what.'

His Enforcer nods. 'You and me. Always.'

Fervently, that is all Kitt Azer wants in this life he now slips from.

Death watches them spar long into the morning. Kitt, the lesser of the two swordsmen, forgets to dodge several of the Enforcer's rehearsed attacks. So, they carry on until every movement is precise. Mara wonders if this is intention, if the king purposely fumbles his footing just to spend more time with his beloved brother.

It is a long while before Kai steps from the ring to carry on with his Enforcer duties. The king, noticing Death for the first time, offers her a breathless smile. His hair is ruffled by the wind's cool fingers, skin slick with sweat. He looks uniquely alive in this moment, despite the obvious tells of Life itself slowly fleeing him.

'What do you know about him?' Mara asks, nodding to the retreating Enforcer.

Kitt chuckles, then coughs. 'Kai? He is my brother.'

'So how much do you know about him?'

'He's a Wielder – a rare Elite able to use the powers of those around him,' the king supplies. 'We share – *shared* – a father. And I know everything about him.' Kitt's smile fades. Mara regrets her question. 'I know everything about Kai, and I would do anything for him. I *am* doing everything for him. This is all for us.'

'Very well.'

The king has grown more irritable as of late, so Death ceases her inquiries. Besides, learning of Kai's *Wielder* ability is all Mara needs to mull over. Her suspicions are nearly confirmed.

'Why do you ask?' Kitt finally sighs out.

Mara watches the Enforcer disappear into a swarm of Imperials. 'So you were born from different wombs?'

'My mother died giving birth to me,' the king admits. 'So, yes. Different queens.'

'Hmm.'

'You choose now to be cryptic, Mara?'

Death is often motivated by the hope of him saying her name.

'I don't choose,' she returns. 'It is simply my nature.'

Mara strides from the king then – she learned a long time ago that it is best to leave a man wanting. She can feel those green eyes tracing her figure (Death has left her cloak in the Mors, you see – not for Kitt, of course, but because it is unseasonably warm). Following her usual routine, Mara ensures to check on her other two souls. Quite the motherly creature she is.

When Death appears behind the Tele's locked door, she finds the floor to be scattered with candles. 'Okay,' Lenny is saying, 'so you'll have me pinned against the wall like the hopeless Hyper I am, and when Pae isn't looking, you let me go—'

'So you can tip a candle and start the fire I die in.' Blair rolls her eyes. 'Yeah, I got it.'

The Imperial surveys the room and every candle discreetly decorating it.

'I'll need to get some cooking oil from the kitchen to sprinkle on the floor.'

Mara weaves through the sea of wax before taking a seat on the bed, thoroughly enthralled. She had not expected to walk in on such scheming.

Blair sighs in annoyance. This is not their first time running through this plan, Death concludes. 'The Ordinary will be trapped in the flames—'

'She won't be *in* the flames,' Lenny cuts in. 'Just . . . surrounded. And I will get her out of the room before she is harmed. This will be perfectly safe,' he adds, more for himself than the Tele.

'She'll be fine,' Blair huffs. 'This is *my* fake death, after all. I'll disappear behind the flames and head down the hidden stairway.'

It is hardly the most impressive plan, but Death, truthfully, had expected worse.

The Imperial nods slowly. 'And I will declare you dead.'

Mara very much dislikes being wrongfully accused.

'What about my body?'

Blair's skepticism is met with a shrug. 'I'll say I took care of it?'

'My mother will ask questions,' the Tele retorts. 'You will have to tell her that my body was severely burned, so you buried me in the cemetery before anyone could see. We have a family plot there. The sergeant will be relieved that you spared her the embarrassment of holding a funeral.'

'What could she possibly be embarrassed about?' Lenny asks, baffled. 'She would have just lost her daughter. Well, not actually, but still.'

'Death by Ordinary,' she states. 'She will be crippled by the shame.' The Tele smiles sinisterly. 'That is one of the reasons I find this plan so enticing.'

'Right.' Lenny clears his throat. Then, with a slight tilt of his head, he murmurs, 'Speak of the devil . . .'

Mara hears it several seconds later, that incessant clicking of heels. Blair barely manages to roll her eyes before the door is swiftly unlocked and swung open. 'This is ridiculous,' the sergeant declares. She strides towards Blair with all the confidence of a woman twice her stature. 'You've hid from the Ordinary long enough. It's time to resume your studies so you don't disgrace us all when your father steps down.'

Blair holds her mother's steely stare.

Lenny watches, hesitantly.

And Death, well, she quite enjoys a good show.

'I think I'll stay in here, actually,' the Tele retorts simply.

'Don't be coy,' her mother snaps. She then grabs Blair's wrist and begins dragging her towards the door. 'And stop picking at your palm,' she orders, examining her daughter's hand. 'Such a nasty habit—'

Mentally, Blair slams the door shut before yanking her arm from the sergeant's grasp.

'Too imperfect for you?' Blair sneers. Her mother turns, slowly, to face her daughter's disdain. 'When I was seven,' she starts slowly, 'my fingers were bandaged for a month. At age ten, you tied gloves around my wrists. All because you couldn't have people seeing I was damaged.'

'Enough,' the sergeant spits. 'You ungrateful child. I always knew you would be an utter disgrace—'

'You can't speak to her like that.'

Mara turns on her heel, brows lifting slightly at the Imperial's boldness. Blair seconds this surprise and whips her head in Lenny's direction.

The sergeant seems startled by his presence. It is as though she hadn't even noticed him. 'And why not?'

'Because I have been ordered by the king to guard Blair from any threat,' he says in a shockingly assertive tone. 'And that now includes you.'

The woman blinks. Then she laughs humorlessly. 'Oh, this is pathetic! You are nothing, child. Now stay out of affairs that don't concern you.'

Blair steps forward then, shielding the Imperial with her own body. 'I'm the only one who gets to be a bitch to him,' she sneers.

'Yeah,' Lenny agrees from over her shoulder. 'What she said.'

'Now get out, Mother.' The door swings open at the Tele's command. 'I told you. I'm staying here.'

The sergeant's gaze flicks between the two souls, now further entangled. Death is peering at the mingling of gold and green when the woman huffs in disbelief. It really is rather obvious where Blair came from. 'I don't believe it,' she murmurs towards her daughter. 'You care for him.'

The Tele grows very still. 'I do not.'

Another biting laugh from the sergeant, this one followed by the retreating click of her heels. 'You know better than to lie to me, Blair.' She stops in the doorway, bristling. 'Rot in here if you like. You have already disgraced this family enough.'

And with that, the sergeant leaves a deafening silence in her wake.

Mara eyes the Tele and her Imperial. Unknowingly, she has begun tapping her foot against the floor.

'She's a Bluff,' Lenny murmurs. 'Isn't she?'

(Death finds the title of this Elite to be rather self-explanatory.)

Blair slams the door shut once again. 'It doesn't mean anything.'

'Oh, yes it does.' The Imperial laughs in disbelief. 'It means you care about me, and that is the truth.'

'The truth,' Blair says in that patronizing tone, 'is that I will snap you in half, gingersnap.'

'See, your heart is racing, which makes me think you're lying—'

The Tele launches that purple ball at his face once again (Mara still does not understand where it keeps coming from), effectively shutting him up.

Death almost smiles at the unlikely pair.

Perhaps not all entangled souls are doomed. Yes, these two are different. They are soul ties, Mara supposes — free to decide what they are to each other. Alongside the other is precisely where they are meant to be.

Surely, this is the case for Death and a certain soul who warms her cold heart.

CHAPTER 20

Ritt

The blades of grass look sharp beneath the streaming moonlight.

Death sits beside me in the field beyond the gardens, and it's oddly comforting, her closeness. I know I shouldn't feel at ease beside the woman who will soon drag me to the Mors, but it feels *quiet* in her presence. Like my weary soul is sighing.

The vile tonics Eli forces down my throat each day are doing precisely as much as Mara predicted they would – nothing. My head pounds incessantly, and I find most everyone to be intolerable. In other words, the Plague is slowly killing me from the inside out.

But with Death, I feel most alive. Every ache is dulled in her presence. In fact, I could almost forget about my imminent demise.

'Do you know why you are dying?'

Within a puddle of moonlight, Mara's stoic features look as though they are cut from marble. I sigh at the question and tell her what she likely wishes to hear. 'Because of my greed?'

'Of course. But not entirely.' She unfurls her legs atop the soft grass, displaying the fitted pants hugging them. The cloak that usually smothers her figure has mysteriously gone missing. 'Greedier men have lived long and prosperous lives.'

I look up at the inky sky. 'So, why is it I'm dying, Mara?'

'Because you, and everyone else in this kingdom, are ignorant to power,' she states.

My lips pull into a frown. 'I know my power.'

'You know how to wield what you were given.' Death leans on the pair of palms she places behind her back. It's a casual movement that equally does and doesn't suit her. 'But you do not know the power.'

I consider this. 'And you do?'

'Quite personally.'

'Is that why you died?' I ask before thinking better of it. 'Power?'

She stares at me with the deep knowingness of someone who was forced to discover everything on their own. I'm not sure I like that look. Death may know me entirely, but I could not even wager a bet as to what she is thinking at any given moment.

Then, slowly enough to quicken my heartbeat, she says, 'I

am all that was, and all that will soon come to pass. But before that, I was in love.'

I swallow, relieved to be right about one thing.

Mara was not always Death.

'Is love not a power of its own?' I murmur.

'For those lucky enough.' Her voice is even. It always is. 'But for most, it means certain death.'

I can't help but stare at her. Death's profile is somehow soft and striking beneath the starry sky. The most terrifying thing about her is the way in which she speaks, with poise and conviction. And every time she opens her mouth, I find myself agreeing with the words that fall from it.

Love, too, has brought me certain death.

All of this, all that I am, is because I loved a man who didn't even understand the meaning of such a word.

Now I am a monster, a king, a bit of both.

Now I no longer trust love, my heart. Not with anyone but my brother.

Crickets chirp all around, filling the silence with their songs. The night air is crisp. She really should be wearing that cloak. If Death were just a girl, and I were just a boy, I might have offered her my jacket.

'So—' I clear my throat '—you promised to tell me about the souls.'

It is pointless to ask Mara any more about her death – or rather, her speculated life. Anything she wanted to say, she would have told me already. And I have no interest in testing Death's patience.

'Yes.' She seems deep in thought. Really, she always seems that way, and consequently, it always feels as though I am disrupting her. 'I can shift my perspective to the spiritual plane. Seeing one's soul helps me better understand the type of person they are.'

I cross my ankles and mirror Mara's deceivingly relaxed position. The grass is damp beneath my palms. 'When you say you can see souls, that means what, exactly?'

'It's like a mass of energy,' she supplies. 'Every human is unique. There are different colors and shapes and even movements.'

I cough into a fist and try to ignore Death literally looking over my shoulder. 'So,' I finally manage, 'what does mine look like?'

'Blue,' she answers softly. 'Muted. Like a puddle reflecting a dimming sky.'

'And the shape?'

'An oval.'

I frown slightly. 'That doesn't seem very interesting.'

'It's not, really,' Mara states in that blatant matter. Then she shrugs stiffly, like a person who's forgotten how to execute the gesture. 'I've seen a lot of souls.'

I chuckle, and she almost returns the sound with a slight smile. 'Good to know I'm average, thank you.'

Death holds me in her gaze for a long moment. 'And there is little movement,' she says finally. 'Your soul is fading.'

I draw a deep breath, but most importantly, I do not dwell. 'Right, well, what does my soul say about me?'

'Typically,' she starts evenly, 'the darker the color, the more troubled the person — their past, their virtue, their mind. This isn't always the case, though. For you . . .' Mara hesitates for the first time. It's strangely human of her. 'Your soul seeks companionship. There is a sadness within you.'

There is no point in denial, so I let my silence speak for itself.

I have always known of this darkness within me. It was felt for the first time at the age of four when discovering that it was I who killed my mother. And I might have unleashed that *something* within me if it weren't for the fact that Kai was deemed the calculated, cold brother, and I the caring and kind one. So I buried that kernel of sadness somewhere deep within me. And when Father died, uprooting that part of myself, it looked a bit madder than I remembered.

'Kitt?'

My gaze snaps to Mara's. It's strange, hearing Death utter your name. 'Sorry,' I murmur. 'Just thinking.'

'Stay with your thoughts.' She dips her head. 'I'll be here when you're done.'

I almost refuse her offer for the sake of being polite. Then, a smile tempts my lips.

No one, living or dead, has ever offered to wait outside my thoughts for me. So I shut my eyes and ponder beside her.

After the passing of several peaceful minutes, I ask, hesitantly, 'Do you still need time with your thoughts?'

'I'm always with my thoughts,' Mara returns. 'But I can free myself of them for now.'

I look up at the smattering of stars. 'What does Death think about? If you don't mind me asking.'

'Mostly the living.' She lifts her gaze to rest it beside mine. 'But tonight, I'm thinking about why you are marrying a woman you hate.'

'I don't hate Paedyn,' I say sharply. My head is beginning to pound once again. 'In fact, I had dinner with her this evening.' I recall vaguely how distracted she seemed. 'And before everything, we were even . . . close. Now she is my peace offering to the other kingdoms so they will open their borders for trade.'

Mara looks unimpressed. 'And you will then infect the cities with this *Plague* you know nothing about?'

'I've already started,' I say quickly.

This manages to crack her stony facade. 'Izram.'

I nod. 'The crate of roses Paedyn left as a gift are sprinkled with a diluted dose of the Plague. Once one person falls ill—'

'The rest will follow,' Death states. 'Mirroring what happened a century ago.'

'Exactly.' My words swell with surety. 'And the kingdoms

will soon thank me for the power I have given them.'

'Hmm.' Mara gives no indication of her thoughts on this matter. 'That still doesn't explain your dislike for Paedyn Gray.'

I shut my eyes against a wave of irritability. 'It's not her, necessarily. It's Kai. I only want Kai, but he wants her. He . . .' My chest tightens painfully. It's difficult to breathe, but I spit out the words furiously. 'He can't love her more. This is all for us. I . . . I need him to choose me.'

'Your Majesty!'

My head throbs in time to my racing heart. I whip around, finding an Imperial racing towards me. Still, Mara watches me with those sharp eyes, a wave of questions likely sitting on the tip of her tongue.

'Your Majesty,' the Imperial pants as he nears our patch of grass. I straighten instinctively. My eyes flick to where Death sits beside me. It is strange, being the only one bearing witness to her presence.

The young man skids to a stop in the dewy grass.

'There's a fire in the castle, Your Majesty.'

CHAPTER 21

Mara

Death does not feel the sweltering heat she steps into.

Flames ripple along the floorboards Mara frequently sat on, shrouding the window she so loved to look out. The room is cast in a destructive glow, thick smoke hangs in the air. But this all seems rather tame when compared to the grappling figures surrounded by fire.

The future queen has pinned a weakened Tele to the floor.

An Imperial shouts behind a wall of hungry flames.

It seems Blair Archer's death has gone awry.

Mara encircles the tense scene sprawled atop a scorched floor. The two women remain within the ring of fire – skin burned, and hair singed. Paedyn's knees dig into the Tele's blistered forearms, forcing a scream from her lips.

It seems the Ordinary (who is anything but with that look

of cruel detachment) is shoving Blair's ashen face towards the wall of flame.

Death has not anticipated such brutality from the bride-to-be. Perhaps she will not go through with such a vicious act. But Mara recognizes the look on her face, for revenge always remains the same, no matter the features it is displayed on. Even as smoke fills her lungs and consciousness begins to fade, Paedyn knows only the vengeance burning within her.

'Please,' Blair whimpers.

Paedyn pushes her closer to the flame.

'Please . . .'

The Imperial is shouting again. The fire swells higher.

But Death only has eyes for the girl who has continually evaded her.

'I told you,' the future queen says hoarsely, blue eyes never straying from the terror filling the Tele's, 'I would make you beg.'

A splitting scream fills the hazy air when the side of Blair's face meets fire.

Skin bubbles, and the sickening smell of it lingers.

Paedyn Gray does not so much as flinch.

Mara thinks, in another lifetime, she would make a fine Death.

Then, with a ragged cough, the human collapses.

Death stares at the bleak scene before her. She crouches, slowly, beside the gasping Tele – pain and adrenaline are all that keep her conscious. A crude line from her temple to chin is carved out in flayed flesh. The skin is blistered, oozing in a way that makes even Mara grimace.

Yet again, she is unsure what to do with this soul that now teeters on her lifeline.

Just as it had during that fight in the slums, a tangible connection forms between Blair and Death. It is fading now, seeing that the Tele is no longer directly in harm's way, but Mara clings to that slippery tether between them.

Once, she might have let Fate have her way with this soul. But Death has recently been reminded what it is like to live (perhaps for the love of another). You see, Mara no longer wishes to stand idly by. She will do what was not done for her.

'You need to get up,' she says simply.

Blair's bleary gaze widens when it lands on the face of Death, who uses every bit of the power she possesses (on this plane) to force a foothold here, in this moment, with this soul.

Tears stream down the Tele's face. She fails to form words.

Lenny bursts through the wall of flames with a yelp, having finally found a dying pocket in the fiery hedge. 'You need to get up, Blair!' He wraps his arms around the unconscious Ordinary, hoisting her into the singed sleeves of his uniform. 'Please!' With one final plea, he staggers through the flames once more, carrying his future queen to safety.

Death turns her attention back to the whimpering Blair.

'He's right. You can stay here and die in this castle – if not now, then after a long life of bitterness. Or you can stand up and live. The choice is yours, Blair Archer. But if I had the chance to choose my fate all over again,' she says sternly, 'I would choose Life, not Death.'

The Tele stares at Mara, equally terrified and determined.

Then she squeezes her eyes shut and nods. The movement has her crying out in pain, but she pushes past it and into a sitting position. Tears seep into her charred skin, and still, she stands on shaking limbs.

Lenny has returned, shoving through the fire once again. 'You're okay!' he shouts, wrapping an arm around Blair. She nearly collapses against him. 'I've got you!'

Death's connection to the Tele's soul flickers out, banishing her to solitude once again. But she watches, exactly as she has and likely always will. The pair lean on each other as they stumble across the sweltering room. Lenny shields his assignment as best he can, though not at the king's command but of his own volition.

Shouts ring in the distance. The king – who Mara abandoned in the field to appear within the fiery room – has finally caught up with her. And he has brought a gaggle of guards with him.

The Imperial yanks aside the fireplace's stone backing. 'Get to the tunnel,' he instructs, helping Blair onto the staircase below. 'I will deal with this and meet you down there. Then we will figure this out.'

The Tele refuses to look at him. She turns her marred face away.

The parade of pounding boots grows closer.

Lenny extends a shaking hand towards her. His fingers brush the unblemished side of her chin, lifting it gently until Blair's watery eyes meet his. 'I'm so sorry.' His voice cracks. 'This shouldn't have happened to you.'

A tear rolls down the Tele's blistered cheek. She is little more than an empty vessel, void of any and all emotion. Even Death is not capable of such bleakness.

A charred beam falls from the ceiling and splinters into sparks behind them. Lenny whips around, covering his face from the debris.

And when he turns back to face the soul now tied to his own, she is gone.

They are eerily quiet, this Tele and Imperial.

Death believes this is the longest they have gone without a word to satiate the silence.

The tunnels are quite cold and damp, even by Mara's standards. The flickering lantern Lenny has carried down the winding steps paints the rounded walls in dancing shadows. Blair sits stiffly beside Death (unbeknownst to her, of course) with a constant welling of tears in her eyes.

Clearing his throat, the Imperial uncorks a glass vial. 'I'm sorry I wasn't here sooner,' he murmurs. 'I had to deal with burying your fake body, then my uncomfortable conversation with the king and his fuming Enforcer. But your night has been far worse, so I should probably stop talking.' He sighs before dumping the dark contents of that vial onto a rumpled shirt. 'I swiped a healing salve from the infirmary. They will definitely notice it's gone missing since they are pretty hard to come by, but that is a problem for another day.'

Blair says nothing.

Hesitantly, Lenny lifts the cloth towards her. 'Uh . . . May I?'

The Tele slowly pulls her face from the shadows in silent permission. A gentle stream of light skims the angry, red burns marring the side of Blair's face. It's strange, seeing the once-soft skin draped in such misfortune, now blistered and swollen.

Death knows pain, and this is it.

Lenny swallows at the gruesome sight. 'This salve should heal, but it will hurt.'

Again, Blair says nothing in response but winces when the salve meets her seared skin.

'I'm sorry.' Free from the mask, the Imperial's face plainly displays his despair. 'It wasn't meant to happen this way. I didn't think Paedyn would—'

'Don't,' Blair grinds out.

A tear rolls down her cheek, mingling with the salve there.

'Right.' Lenny nods, saddened. 'Yeah, I'm sure you don't want to talk about it.'

Mara sits comfortably within the heavy silence that follows. She watches (in awe, though she wouldn't admit it) as the ointment seeps into the burned flesh to heal it from the inside out. The bubbled blisters begin to smooth; the raw skin starts to dull.

It's not long before Death grows bitter at the miraculous sight. You see, a lifetime ago, Healers didn't have the luxury of cheating with powerful potions.

The Imperial clears his throat in warning of the words about to leave his lips. 'Though it pains me to say it, you were right. Your mother was happy I buried you before anyone saw.' He draws a deep breath. 'And by you, I mean the several pillows I rolled into a blanket and carried from your burning bedroom. The Imperials outside didn't argue when I said I had to take care of the body.'

When this earns no response, Lenny smiles weakly. 'So . . . you're dead. Congrats.'

'No,' Blair whispers. 'I'm ruined.'

'Ruined?' The Imperial practically laughs in her face. 'Blair, you look like a badass. I'm a little jealous.'

With the salve numbing her pain, the Tele freely expresses her annoyance. 'The only thing worth liking about me was my appearance,' she snaps. 'Even with this ointment, I'm still marred for life.'

Lenny looks at her, *really* looks at her. Mara finds herself envious of such delicate regard. Once, she knew what it felt like to be on the receiving end of such beholding. But she has long forgotten.

'I brought you something else,' the Imperial finally says. Reaching into one of the many pockets of his singed uniform, he pulls free a bundled napkin. Mara leans in to watch him unravel it and display a pair of glistening desserts. 'Lemon tarts,' he presents proudly. 'To celebrate. And they probably aren't as good as yours, but at least mine were made with joy and shit.'

Yes, Death recalls that night in the kitchen quite fondly. Threats were thrown, along with several ingredients. But these desserts are not the product of that evening (those lemon tarts were swiftly eaten, of course). Mara is a bit embarrassed that she hadn't known about the Imperial's sly baking excursion. Though, she has been rather distracted as of late, justifiably so.

'You . . . baked these?' Blair grinds out in disbelief.

The Imperial beams. 'Pretty impressive, huh?'

'Not in the slightest,' the Tele retorts. 'The crust is so dry it's a choking hazard. And let me guess, you stirred the glaze with a ladle instead of a spoon.'

'Do they not do the same thing?' Lenny's eyes dart from her narrowed gaze before returning worriedly. 'Stir?'

It is like reliving that night in the kitchen, Mara concludes. She now finds it remarkable, how easily they conceive these pointless disputes. But she can see, more astutely than most, that their constant bickering has become so much more. For it is a language of their very own, a union of souls.

'Whatever,' Lenny concedes. 'That's beside the point.' He

lifts the napkin between them, crumbs showering his lap. 'I made these, and I like them. Not because of their appearance or the concerningly dry crust, which was definitely intentional. But because they are tart, just like you.'

'I'm sour.' Blair's correction is quick. 'You will just spit me out like everyone else.'

'You're an acquired taste.' The Imperial's gaze grows beseeching in the flickering light. 'And so much more than a pretty face – which you still have. You are funny, even when it's at my expense, and smart in a hurtful, belittling sort of way. But above all—' he pauses to take a breath '—you are strong. And this is your chance to be whoever you want, so . . .' Lenny turns the Tele's face towards him with the tips of his fingers. 'Be the girl with the badass scar.'

The words are genuine, and yet, Death notes how utterly terrified Lenny sounds when saying them. That strange intrigue he feels for this Tele has further nudged its way towards his heart. But Blair Archer with her prickly nature is hardly the best place to plant any sort of affection. For she will surely choke the life from him.

And yet, something within them is drawn to the other, barbs and all.

Their souls are laced – like that of friends, but perhaps more.

Blair draws a sudden breath. Her brown eyes are wide, searching her gingersnap's (Death likes to think this is now an endearing nickname) with a fervor that seems to paralyze him.

Jostled from her trance, the Tele snatches one of those crumbling tarts from the napkin. 'Right, well, in case you've forgotten, I don't care what you think.'

Lenny can't help but smile as Blair abruptly returns to her snide self. 'Of course you don't.'

'Exactly.'

'Great.'

'Good.'

'Hmm.' The Imperial frowns. 'I was planning on saying "good" next, so you kind of ruined our back-and-forth here—'

He is cut off by a dramatic vocalization of Blair's disdain. 'I'm so glad I'm dead, so I can be rid of you.'

'Right.' Lenny's smile fades. He had forgotten about the separation part of this plan, Mara thinks. 'And I haven't been thrown out of the castle yet, so that's something.'

'It will only be a matter of time,' Blair reassures. 'You're a horrible Imperial.'

'Hey, you wanted me to let you be killed.'

His words spark the Tele's memory. 'I saw someone in that room. A woman.'

Death straightens. She is rarely mentioned so directly in conversation. The inclusion is quite nice. She finds herself smoothing the hair neither of them can see.

Lenny lifts a brow. 'What?'

'She told me to get up,' Blair reminisces, her brow creased. 'I had never seen her before. She just . . . appeared. Whatever.'

She rolls her eyes. 'I probably imagined it.'

Mara was hoping for a bit more detail about her cameo in the land of the living, but this would suffice. She leaves the souls there in that dark tunnel, conversing closely. Because there is not much more for her to witness, Death realizes. She started such spying in the hopes of disaster – and they have greatly disappointed.

Mara was wrong.

She is unused to the feeling. And the admittance of it.

Then, Death believed every bond to be doomed.

Lover. Friend. Foe.

Now, a certain soul has begun to change her mind.

Some, you see, are just meant to be.

I try not to think about that, though. I am simply doing what needs to be done, what greatness demands.

I am not a monster.

Beyond each row of windows, the sun slinks shyly towards the horizon, leaving behind a night of long-winded condolences and vile tonics on my tongue. Each step grows heavier than the last. I'm being betrayed by my very body, and Death is witnessing my demise.

'Are you going to tell him?' Mara asks.

I glance over at her. 'Tell Kai what?'

'That you are dying.'

I look away, my heart now pounding harder than my head.

'He deserves to know,' she adds evenly.

'Not yet,' I say too quickly. 'I'm . . . I'm not ready.'

Mara says nothing more on our short journey – she doesn't need to. Her previous words are damning enough. And when I come to a stop before my beloved brother's door, I realize that I have never feared Death, only the imminent likelihood of losing my brother to Life.

'Are you going inside?' Mara's gaze is heavy.

I look down to find my hand hovering over the doorknob. Hazily, I nod and turn the handle.

Kai stands before a battered bedpost, a sword in hand. It is comforting to know that some things never change.

'Oh, good,' I say at the sight of him. 'You're awake.'

His room is familiar, but I step tentatively inside. When we were boys, and a harsh storm rattled the windows, we would slide beneath the bed and eat whatever sweets we had swiped from the kitchen. Now those memories feel so delicate.

Kai raises the blade in his hand. 'Just blowing off some steam.'

Death pads into the room where she examines the chipped bedpost further, then stares pointedly at the wardrobe behind the brothers.

'Right.' My mind is drifting again. It has been doing that of late, mostly without warning.

What if he hates me for this? What if I fail, and everything I've done is for nothing? What if he chooses her?

Words begin falling from my numb lips. 'Well, I just wanted to stop in and let you know that the third Trial will be taking place tomorrow.'

The look of surprise he dons is . . . unsurprising.

My head hurts.

'Tomorrow?' he asks. 'You're not announcing it to the court?'

I swipe a palm across the back of my neck. Father used to do the same thing. But I don't want to be like him. Am I like him? 'It's meant to be . . . unexpected,' I manage. 'For Paedyn, at least. It will take place in the Bowl.'

'I see.'

Kai is watching me closely.

So is Death. She stands beside him.

They wear a similar expression, like the look of pity that something pathetically fragile earns.

I am not fragile – not like Father said.

I will be everything he thought I couldn't be—

'Kitt, are you all right?'

'Hmm?' I intend to focus my gaze on Kai, but it falls to Mara instead.

She now stands behind him, having begun to circle my Enforcer. Her voice is steady. 'Tell him, Kitt.'

'No. No, not yet. It's not time . . .' I find myself murmuring back. '. . . I need the right time . . .'

Kai takes a slow step towards me after glancing over his shoulder. 'What? Kitt, is everything okay?'

The concern in his voice urges me to wrangle my muddled thoughts. That constant din inside my skull suddenly quiets. I blink. Even smile. 'Yes, no need to worry. It seems I need some more sleep.' Then I think about that final Trial, and my worry returns. 'Just . . . just trust me. I have everything under control.'

My brother nods without hesitation. 'Of course. I trust you with my life.'

A slightly ironic choice of words, considering tomorrow's events.

I fail to swallow my cough, so I follow it with a bright smile. 'I've never doubted that about you.'

Mara trails me to the door. My thoughts begin to diffuse, and still, I know one thing. 'You and me, Brother.'

'You and me.'

I step out into the hall with Death on my heels. If she bothered displaying any emotion, I imagine it would be concern, just like everyone else who lays eyes on me. For that reason, her stoicism is a relief.

'I didn't have the chance to teach you how to die,' she says simply as we stride through the shadowy hallway. 'We were interrupted.'

'Right . . .' It has grown rather difficult to focus. 'You didn't.'

Mara stops abruptly, so I do the same. 'Perhaps when you are better prepared,' she ventures, 'you will be able to tell your brother.'

Unlikely.

'Okay,' I appease. 'Show me how to die.'

A flicker of some unreadable emotion softens her features. 'I will.'

She extends a hand.

It is small, her palm uncalloused.

Death is terrifyingly unassuming.

A bit apprehensively, I place my much larger hand in hers.

'This might feel a bit uncomfortable,' she says absentmindedly. 'Like your stomach dropping.'

'What—?'

Before I can even protest, it's happening, precisely as she said. The ground is sinking beneath my feet, and my stomach is plunging with it. I feel tugged in two directions, maybe two dimensions, before my feet collide with solid ground.

Cool air caresses my cheeks; darkness greets my gaze. 'What . . .' I swallow, feeling slightly sick – well, more so than usual. 'What the hell was that?'

'I didn't think you would want to walk all the way to Loot.'

Mara strides casually into the darkness my eyes now slowly adjust to. I'm suddenly standing on the edge of a rundown street in the slums, blinking in disbelief. 'How did we get here?'

Death turns in the center of this quiet street. 'We stepped between different points on this plane.' She says this like one might when commenting on the weather. 'I focused the little power I possess in this realm and brought you with me.'

I look up at the night sky where a ceiling resided mere moments before. Then my gaze is back on the embodiment of Death, standing so comfortably in a puddle of moonlight. 'You mentioned your power before – in the gardens.' I step before her. Strangely, I feel my best when we are alone. 'What are you capable of, Mara?'

The corners of her lips twitch, surprising me. 'Everything.'

I raise my brows at her. 'Everything?'

'Nothing I can do is unfamiliar to you.' She says this like I'm supposed to understand.

'So, where did all your power come from?' I ask, attempting a different question.

'The Mors.' Mara taps her foot against the ground, softly. 'It supplies me with anything I need. So when I am parted from it, my power is limited.'

'But,' I start slowly, 'where did the Mors obtain such strength?'

Death stares at me, subtly intrigued. I think she finds my lack of knowledge comical. 'The Mors is all that was, and all that will soon come to pass,' she finally says. 'Its power is not devised or created. It is infinite.'

I nod, despite my continued lack of understanding.

She turns towards a slatted shack then, pointing to the twining trees beside it. Their gnarled branches curl around one another, chalky in color and brittle in the soft breeze. It's impossible to tell where one trunk begins and the other ends. 'This is where Destiny met Fate and Death was born.' Mara's voice grows soft. 'Where eternity began.'

Again, I'm not entirely sure I understand. But I get the sense that her riddle wasn't meant wholly for me. 'Those look like the trees in the Mors,' I say, rather than asking another question she likely won't answer.

'Yes.' Her gaze grows distant. 'They do.'

A dozen dull taps of her foot pass before she finally looks at me and utters a single word. 'Gently.'

'Gently?' I echo.

'That is how to die.'

I can't help but cough out a laugh. 'I thought it was the

opposite. Am I not supposed to fight until the very end?'

'Most do,' she answers evenly. 'But a struggling soul is quite pointless. When one's fate is sealed, hope is only a hindrance.'

'So you truly hope for nothing?' I find myself asking.

'Hope is for the living.'

The strain in her voice saddens me. My connection with Mara may only be due to the imminent demise she will soon drag me to, but it feels real, nonetheless. Like a companion I've searched my whole life for, only to find her in Death. 'Then . . .' I shrug. Shake my head. 'I will be your heartbeat.'

A wave of emotion crashes against Mara's solid mask. 'What?'

'As of right now, I am still living,' I remind her. 'So, hope vicariously through me. If it is a heartbeat hope needs, then I will be that for you.'

She blinks a pair of wide, brown eyes at me. 'No one has ever . . .' Her throat bobs. 'Thank you.'

I smile sadly. 'Even Death deserves to hope.'

'You don't have to go gently,' Mara practically blurts. I've never seen someone so softly flustered. 'Die how you wish. I will catch you, however you fall from your lifeline.'

I ponder this. 'Is it easier for you? If I do not struggle?'

'Infinitely.'

'Then it is decided.' My gaze lifts to the stars above. 'I will go gently. For you.'

When my eyes finally fall back on Death, I almost don't believe what I'm seeing.

She is smiling.

CHAPTER 23

Kitt

Dull petals drift down like ashes on the wind.

Like an omen I should heed.

Instead, I let the drizzle of decay nestle into my hair and caress my face. A few stubborn blossoms still cling to the twining branches above despite the wind's incessant tugging. Once, the flowers were vibrant, thrumming with life before the bitter chill set in. Before the death of everything I knew.

Perhaps there is an odd parallel there, one I don't care to explore at the moment.

I quicken my pace along the path when that familiar panic begins its swell in my chest. This, mercifully, has the throng of smothering Imperials falling behind. I don't need them to witness their king's weakness.

My ears ring as I stagger into the Bowl's menacing shadow,

muffling the excitement that echoes within. A shuddering cough rattles my chest and aching body. That unnatural *thing* writhes within me, coiling around the core of my Dual ability until the very essence of me is choking. I'm suddenly gasping for air, bracing a hand against one of the arena's tunneled entrances. It feels as though my soul is being cleaved in half.

I look up to find Death staring back. Sympathetic, she reaches for me—

'Your Majesty!'

The Imperial's shout severs my connection to the Plague searing my veins. I shake my head, trying to free myself of the pained trance. 'I'm fine.' My weak reassurance is ground out between gritted teeth. I cough again, and this time, it tastes of blood.

Straightening, I stride into the stone tunnel with the little composure I've mustered. Imperials nip at my heels, prickling my back with a dozen leery gazes.

They think I'm weak. Just as I have been my entire life.

The sinister thought slithers across my mind without warning. My very power feels as though it's on edge, every emotion heightened and violently tipping towards agitation.

'. . . should recover before addressing the people, Your Majesty?'

My gaze snaps to the masked figure.

An Imperial is questioning my well-being like a pestering Healer. As if I were the gentle prince before, and not the great king now. He has no idea of the power that runs through my veins.

My head pounds.

Weak. Weak. Weak.

Something snaps within me. 'Insinuate I am anything but a god again, and you will pray fervently for my forgiveness.'

The Imperial's jaw slackens, his mouth working until a mumbled 'Of course, Your Majesty' tumbles out.

I blink back the blinding rage, feeling unsteady on my feet.

What the hell just happened?

The fleeting hysteria is a hazy memory I fight to grasp hold of. My mind reels until it's suddenly pondering what I'm meant to be panicking over. I sway there for a moment, head clear as I mentally shrug aside whatever it was that had my heart racing.

'Why are we standing here?' The Imperials blink at my exasperation. 'I have a final Trial to commence.'

And with that, I head into the belly of the Bowl.

My body hums with power as all of Ilya welcomes their king. I sweep my gaze over the roaring crowd, feeling stronger than I ever have before. I raise a hand in greeting as I stride over to my glass box, each step amplified a thousandfold by the stomping of feet surrounding me.

After slipping into the cozy enclosure, I ease gently into the cushioned seat within. My gaze flicks back to the rowdy arena as my fingers drum a steady beat against the plush arm of my chair. The Pit stretches below me; a sea of sand speckled by four bodies. Their white robes are stark against the stone wall, though only three bear the ability that earns them a Sight's garb.

This is the beginning of the end.

I shift uncomfortably in my seat.

No turning back now.

The pounding in my head returns when Paedyn steps into the arena. Incidentally, my heart ceases its necessary pounding when she turns to look at me. Calum has slipped into the box, his gaze heavy on the back of my neck as I stand abruptly, instinctually, at Paedyn's presence. Perhaps because I know this may be the last time I'm in it. Her eyes plead to find something in mine – faith, forgiveness, friendship, *something*. I open my mouth, futilely fumbling for a suitable farewell. Perhaps a 'thank you' for her ignorant part in my legacy. Instead, guilt skewers me in the gut, hard enough to have me bracing a hand against the glass.

I don't feel for her, not in the way I used to. Not in the way Kai still does. No, Paedyn Gray is now nothing more than a pawn in a game she doesn't know exists.

But I'm not sure it's possible to loathe something so resiliently *alive*.

I straighten before lowering slowly into my seat.

Still, I have to try.

Calum clears his throat behind me. This reminds me to concentrate on guarding my thoughts from the Mind Reader – a bit too intently. I hardly hear him when he finally asks, 'How are you feeling, Kitt?'

I keep my gaze fixed on the arena beyond. 'Strong.'

'Of course you are.'

'Oh, don't pretend you're not surprised,' I murmur back. 'The Healers expect me to drop dead any moment, and the Scholars can't wait to gloat when I do.' I glance over my shoulder at him. 'But I'm better than ever. So don't hold your breath waiting for me to take my last.'

'Of course, Your Majesty.' Calum tips his head towards an Imperial beyond the glass. 'I only ask because he seems to think you may be losing your mind.'

'What?' I nearly choke on my incredulous laugh.

Calum pulls his arms behind him. 'Yes, apparently there was an incident outside of the Bowl?'

I shake my head at the blatant lie this Imperial has spun to entertain himself. Our walk to the arena was uneventful at best. After emerging from the tunnel of trees, we . . .

Mentally, I frown, like my mind is frustrated by the mere suspicion of a misplaced memory.

I clear my throat. 'We made it into the Bowl just fine.'

With that, I turn away to conclude our clipped conversation. I then watch a swarm of Imperials shove Paedyn towards the Pit before I step out onto the pathway encircling it. Numbly, I stand behind the railing with an Amplifier at my side, her hand pressed gently to my shoulder.

'Welcome, Ilyans, to Paedyn Gray's final Trial.' My words

are hollow as they echo across the arena. 'Here, we will test her brutality.'

I don't remember much of what else I declare, only the draining of color from Paedyn's face. Even that is a blur behind the mask of stoicism I've secured over my features. Kai isn't the only Azer forced to play a part.

Kai.

He is in the Pit now, striding slowly towards Paedyn. She can't bring herself to turn around and meet the fate I have predestined.

But this is not my brother. No, I am doing this *for* my brother.

Makoto Khitan has the chance to rid us of her, despite that admirable resilience. And he very much wanted this opportunity for revenge when I met him in that shadowed alley. So that is what I will use to keep Kai at my side. And yet, my gaze drops when the first scream rips from Paedyn's throat. My shrouded Wielder holds none of that coveted power back, just as he promised in the shadowed alley where we became unlikely allies.

The Ordinary is forced to face the ultimate Elite.

I'm doing this for Kai. For us.

Sand flies up around them, blurring every movement. I squint through the cloud of haze to see Paedyn's bloody form hovering at the end of a blade. My breath catches, and I stand, nearly pressing my face against the glass. Shifting my eyes to the looming screen above, I trace the sad acceptance settling on Paedyn's face. Her whispered words are meant for the man she loves — but he is not who hears them.

I am not a monster. I am not a monster. I am not a monster.

I hold my breath, waiting for that sword to plunge through my betrothed's chest. Instead, I watch something happen; something shift. I witness the exact moment Kai — *Mak* — damns himself by caring for Paedyn Gray.

He isn't the first man to make such a grave mistake.

The Wielder severs his connection to the Tele's ability. And when Paedyn drops to her knees, he bows back.

I shake my head, swallowing a hysterical laugh.

It seems in every instance, in every body, Kai Azer chooses Paedyn Gray.

So when that dagger slides into his chest, the same one that pierced my father's throat, I force myself to watch.

This is what loving Paedyn Gray will earn you — ruin.

And I vow to save my brother from the fate of *her*.

Death is waiting for me in my study.

'I brought his soul to the Mors,' she says.

I take a seat in my father's worn, leather chair. 'He chose her. It wasn't even Kai, and he still chose her.'

'You look worse' is all she says in response. Her bluntness is admirable, if not slightly annoying.

I lift my gaze to where she stands beside the fireplace.

'I've never felt better.'

CHAPTER 24

Mara

Death was surprised when she had to drag Adena's vengeful lover to the Mors.

His was the last soul she had expected to see awaiting her. He was quite unassuming – a Tele in the slums, a Wielder in the arena. But the powerful man did not struggle or beg. No, he had chosen to meet Mara. And it was Paedyn Gray who delivered him to Death.

She now sits on the floor of a cell between two brothers – indefinitely, it would seem. The man lies cold on the floor, his soul no longer tucked beneath the dagger protruding from an unmoving chest. His still features look relieved. For he, unlike most, found peace in this fate.

Mak was his name. Though, he no longer has use for it.

Paedyn mourns this man, quietly and at length. Kai adorns

one side, Kitt the other. The king frequently meets Mara's gaze from where she stands before the bars. She recognizes, indifferently, that this man's demise further stains Kitt's inky palms. But this, and the many other poor decisions he has made, does not perturb Mara. She is Death, after all. Who is she to judge the flaws of a hopeful human?

Besides, her own moral compass is questionable, at best, and this boy is the first to notice her since this eternity began. He is now her true north (a dangerous bestowment of Death's affection). Everything else has faded away.

He is her heartbeat.

Mara does not stay long. This silent gathering around a corpse is quite dull. You see, Death has grown quite numb to grief. She finds it to be pointless, and above all, boring.

Yes, she has other souls to attend to.

Lenny and Blair sit on a lumpy cot in the slums. They have wisely relocated to the Imperial's home and are found splitting a loaf of stale bread.

The Tele looks peeved. This looks promising.

Death takes a seat on the floor before them, like a child preparing to be read an intriguing story.

'I can't believe this is all you can afford.'

'I didn't become an Imperial for the money,' Lenny mutters around a mouthful of dry dough. 'Actually, I did it to help the Resistance.'

'And now that you've failed?' Blair asks, predictably

demeaning. 'You will remain an Imperial because . . . ?'

Said Imperial swallows. Mara watches him mull the question over. 'Huh. I'm not sure.'

'Then quit,' she supplies.

A long moment passes in which they both pick at their portions.

Death's gaze flicks between them. These two are her last resort for entertainment and are, as of now, failing miserably.

'What if I went with you?' Lenny suddenly blurts.

Oh, this will do nicely.

Blair aims her sharp scrutiny at him. 'What?'

'Look—' he turns to face her fully on the thin cot '—we have already decided I'll help get you to Tando. So, what if I . . . stayed there? I don't know what I want, but I could figure it out,' he says hurriedly. 'There is no hierarchy of power there, and I would be closer to Ma—'

'What are you saying, gingersnap?'

The Tele looks terrified. Her chest has halted, hoarding all the breath in her lungs.

Death flicks her wide gaze between the souls. She is very happy with her decision to leave that damp cell when she did.

Timidly, Lenny meets his former assignment's (she is now so much more) piercing gaze. 'I think, maybe, we could be enough life for one another.'

'No. Don't think,' Blair orders. 'Not about me. Don't place your hope in a hollow heart.'

The Imperial shakes his head, now teetering on the verge of annoyance. 'Do you know how I found you in the slums that night you escaped?'

Blair stares at him, her defiance wavering.

'Because even then, I knew you,' Lenny declares. 'Your heart is not hollow. I listen for it in the silence. I find myself trying to memorize its unique pattern and hating that I can't.'

His words are a proverbial shake to the shoulders, and Mara cannot seem to look away.

'Blair, do you understand?' He swallows. 'I would know you by the beat of your heart alone. And I think that should count for something.'

(Mara remembers, bitterly, what it feels like to be on the receiving end of such a declaration. And yet, she has spent this side of eternity searching for any splinter of love – incessant and lodged beneath one's skin. Perhaps to reminisce on why she became Death and determine whether it was worth it.)

Now the Tele's chest heaves as she stares at him in disbelief.

'I'm not asking you to love me,' Lenny continues softly. 'Hell, you don't even need to like me. Not now. And maybe it's some sixth sense talking, but I am drawn to you, Blair Archer – bitch and all.' He laughs helplessly. 'And I don't know what to do with that other than follow the sound of your heartbeat, wherever it may lead me.'

Blair merely blinks at his profession.

Death, for one, was thoroughly moved by the Imperial's

words (though you would never be able to tell by looking at her). She has begun, tentatively, to believe in love again. Not the hollow promises of her past but the earnest companionship of her present. Though these souls hardly burn with an all-consuming love, they may begrudgingly blossom into something close.

'That,' the Tele begins slowly, 'was unsurprisingly stupid.'

'Look, I know how it sounds—'

'But for all the words you've said,' she cuts in, 'those are the only ones I haven't hated hearing.'

A wide grin begins its slow spread across Lenny's lips. 'You feel it too?'

Mara inches closer, her gaze falling on the Tele.

'I didn't say that.'

'Your heart is beating very fast.'

'You can stay in Tando,' Blair bites. 'But if you ever want to be seen with me again, you will need some actual clothes.'

'Deal,' the Imperial concedes.

'Fine,' Blair says curtly. 'When do we leave?'

'Once Paedyn is settled?' Lenny supplies.

'I would expect nothing less.' This sarcasm is accompanied by the rolling of her eyes.

The Imperial, being quite accustomed to her attitude, ignores this. 'I need to talk to her. She should know I'm leaving after the wedding.'

He stands then, stretching his long limbs.

Blair huffs. 'I'll be here.'

'I'll know.'

'By the beat of my heart?' the Tele blurts despite herself.

Lenny turns, throwing a grin over his shoulder. 'I'll follow the sound of it home.'

'Get out.' Blair can hardly smother her smile. Deep down, she is a rather hopeless romantic, Death thinks. 'Before I change my mind about letting you come with me.'

The Imperial does as he is told, leaving with a glowing soul and a giddy grin. Mara feels a bit saddened by the sight, actually. There is little more for her to study. And where a jaded version of her once preyed on this unlikely pair's demise, Death now finds their unique bond annoyingly sweet.

But no matter their fate, Mara will meet them again.

Likely in this Life.

Most assuredly in Death.

CHAPTER 25

I carve every thought onto a page.

Careless splotches of ink threaten to drown the words.

I keep writing.

I need to pry my mind free.

Quiet moment – I need a quiet moment.

Most of my days are forgotten. It's almost a relief.

The Plague is eating away at my mind – don't take my mind – please – it's all I have left.

Do not take my mind.

I blink at the assortment of scribbled words before me.

I don't remember writing them.

This realization has me reaching for a murky vial at the edge of my desk. I swallow the potent contents, though I know it does nothing to help. I'm dying – Death herself has confirmed

it. But pretending this medicine does anything at all helps me feel some semblance of control. Like I'm not drifting in the unknown, sinking into a demise I brought upon myself.

But the lonely abyss that is the Mors will have to wait. Something far more treacherous awaits me today.

I am getting married.

I used to think such a declaration would accompany love. Now I know better.

My stained fingers tug open a drawer to reveal the carved lid of a jewelry box. Dust has curled up between the swirling ridges of Ilya's crest, but the worn wood is still smooth beneath my fingers as I lift it onto the desk.

My gaze flicks over this intimate memento.

Mother and Father are proof of my naivety. I once thought their adoration for each other was unrivaled. But the evidence within Iris Azer's jewelry box says otherwise.

Her disloyalty is damning.

A bastard may sit beneath the crown.

Pain sears through my chest. I cough, tasting blood. My head spins violently—

Then, stillness.

For one, blissful moment.

'Kitt?'

Death is suddenly standing before me.

'Mara,' I breathe. The pain is gone. In fact, I feel quite well. 'Have you come to wish me luck before the wedding?'

She tilts her head – a continual quirk. 'I already did. The surge of power and pain you felt summoned me here.' Her watchful gaze slides over me. 'That was some time ago now.'

'Right,' I say distantly. 'I . . . I know.'

'No, you do not,' Death returns, though her tone is intrigued where another's might sound demeaning. 'You don't remember our conversation.'

I open my mouth to deny the terrifying truth she has stumbled upon when my eyes fall to the empty desk before me. 'Where did the jewelry box go?' I ask slowly. 'It was right here, I—'

'You took it to your betrothed,' Mara supplies. 'I went with you.'

'Why . . . ?' I pinch the bridge of my nose, feeling that splitting headache begin to return. 'Why would I do that?'

Death attempts that almost-shrug of hers. 'Humans are sentimental. You wished for Paedyn to wear a piece of your mother's jewelry.'

The love notes were still in the drawer.

What the hell is wrong with me?

Maybe she will think they are from Father.

'Shit,' I mutter.

I *need* her to think they are from Father.

She cannot know. No one can know.

I am not a bastard. I am a king.

I can't be a bastard. I must be a king.

Monster – what if all I am is a monster—?

'Shit!'

This curse is far louder than the last. I clutch my head, the twining crown piercing my palms, as if that alone could silence the noise within it. My breath is quick and shallow.

Mara simply studies me, unflinchingly. 'Memory loss. The Plague is overpowering you. The living can only handle so much.'

'I'm fine,' I pant.

'Why continue attempting this greatness?' she asks plainly. 'You already know what fate awaits you, and yet, you are to be married.'

My mouth is dry. 'You know why, Mara. This greatness isn't just for me. If I cannot reap the benefits of this new world I am creating, then Kai will. His legacy will be revered.' I smile weakly at the thought. 'I will make sure of that. Because, despite his gruesome role in life, he is not strong enough to do what needs to be done.'

Mara studies me, softer than her typical scrutiny. Her brown eyes flick over my face. They trace my brows, my lips, my flickering soul beneath. There is something strangely intimate about the brushing of Death's gaze.

Chestnut hair slips over cloakless shoulders when she cocks her head at me. 'You are the best this Azer line has to offer. I would know.'

Inky parchment swims before my eyes. 'I think you will

find plenty who disagree when they discover what I've done.'

I drum my fingers against the wooden desk.

Mara takes a slow step forward. She extends a hand that brushes my own. Her touch is cold, startling.

'Most do not appreciate the art of necessary brutality,' she reassures. 'But I am not most. I am all.'

Agony. It cleaves me in half.

Then—

I'm standing before my court. I blink at them from the dais draped in flowers. The queen's crown awaits Paedyn's head beside me.

The doors swing open.

My wedding is sprawled before me, and I don't remember arriving.

Paedyn Gray strides towards me. She looks horrified.

I'm not the brother she wants.

Am I what my brother wants? Or will he choose her, always her, only her—

I grit my teeth. Fight to stay present in this moment.

My fingers toy with the buttons of my elegant tunic.

Paedyn meets me at the altar. I offer her a hand.

My gaze skims over her swiftly, searching for any flash of jewels. But my bride-to-be wears none of Mother's belongings, nor the look of one who discovered a ruinous detail.

She did not find the notes.

The Scholar rattles off a string of sentences I hardly hear.

I'm far too focused on not retreating into my muddled mind.

I say 'I do' when I am told.

I'm surprised when Paedyn manages to choke out the words after me. She really would do anything for a united Ilya. And I will keep that promise.

Soon, we will all be united. As Elites.

I am urged to kiss the bride.

Some part of me figured Kai would burst into the throne room by now. But he doesn't, and that is hope.

I kiss his beloved, swiftly.

Kai doesn't know it yet, but this is for him. For us. Always.

We turn towards the crowd, our fingers interlaced.

I meet Death's gaze in the sea of bodies.

It is fitting that she is here.

A piece of me has just died.

Love is a luxury.

And the naive boy who thought differently is laid to rest in this flowery grave.

CHAPTER 26
Mara

Mara's gaze traces the steady trickle of blood cascading down the stone steps.

It pours from the crumpled man beside her, Life leaking from the wound in his chest. And though Death has a duty to fulfill – gathering this soul for the Mors and whatnot – Mara would like a moment longer to admire such an act of violence that was surely warranted.

Kitt – with a detached ruthlessness that awed even Death – plunged a sword through this man's chest. She had never seen this soul before, but the king had doubtlessly delivered it to her for a reason. It is admirable, Kitt's conviction.

For he and Death are one and the same.

Yes, they do what must be done.

Mara drags the stoic soul into the afterlife while the king

and queen converse in hushed voices. She trudges through the Mors' swampy earth with the happy couple in mind (this is facetious, of course – they look rather miserable together, to her delight). No, Death does not feel threatened by Paedyn Gray. She admires the stubborn soul, that is to be sure. But this Ordinary, as they call those *mysteriously* untouched by the Plague (Mara would have to ask the trees about that), is not fated for this Azer. Rather, her soul is tethered to his brother.

And Kitt's belongs to Death – eternally.

She leaves the disoriented man on a patch of cracked earth.

'. . . he killed me. Me?! I did everything for him, his father . . . And all out of fear he was a bastard?'

A pang of hurt hits Mara in the chest, right where her thawing heart resides.

Kitt had not confided in her.

She blames this lapse in judgment on his fragile mind. For he would have shared something so significant with her – she knows it. Their connection runs deep, unlike anything Death has ever felt (in this lifetime, at least). Such a bond as this is woven into their very beings.

This is fate (and the last man Mara thought this of quickly met his – brutally).

Death is nothing if not obsessive. Every creature is compiled of flaws, and Mara is more aware of hers than most. Her intelligence and insatiable curiosity are only rivaled by these possessive tendencies – nobody is perfect. But she has diligently buried that part of herself for longer than a lifetime, you see, and it has grown rather tiring.

It is not Death's fault that Kitt Azer makes her feel young. Alive. Like she is staring into the face of a lost lover.

Mara spends some time (it is impossible to know how long in the Mors) collecting trapped souls from their cold corpses. Her craft has been rather neglected since her intrigue (infatuation, some might say) with the king. So, Death listens to the griping of every soul she drags, even apologizes for not tending to them sooner. For she is not a monster.

When Mara finally steps back into the land of the living, night has fallen over Ilya. She makes her way to the king's study, rather giddily for Death (and one might even be able to tell from her expression). Kitt is found precisely as he always is, hunched over a pile of parchment and scribbling relentlessly.

'It seems I missed your second wedding,' Mara says by way of greeting. She knew of their plans for a ceremony on Loot. Strange, these humans.

The king doesn't look up from the steady stream of ink he guides across the page. Golden hair sticks up between the woven crown atop his head. He manages only a few muttered words. 'No . . . I have to keep writing . . . before it's too late.'

Hmm. Death seems to have caught him at a bad time. It is the Plague that has hold of his mind now. Or rather, a power Mara knows to be quite dominating. But this brief spell of hysteria hardly deters her. Kitt will soon be free of the Life he grapples with and cling wholly to Death.

'I dragged the soul you killed to the Mors.' Mara takes a seat before the king's desk. 'He seemed less than pleased.'

That cloudiness in Kitt's gaze retreats at the words. He blinks then, as though waking up from a dream.

The king is back. If only for a little while.

'Calum,' he murmurs. His green gaze (Mara's weakness in every lifetime) falls to the ink coating his palms. 'I don't know what came over me. He was a threat and suddenly . . . suddenly, I was running him through with my blade.'

Death's boot taps a steady beat against the worn rug. 'You did not tell me your worry of legitimacy.'

A crease of confusion forms between his brows, right above those eyes Mara has fallen for more than once. 'It was not your burden to bear.'

'What is yours—' Death stares at him pointedly '—is mine. Our eternity begins very soon.'

Kitt visibly fights to stay focused. He shakes his head. Runs a hand down his face. 'What do you mean, *our* eternity?'

'Well, we are fated, of course,' Death says simply. 'You have sacrificed your soul to be with me. We will rule the Mors together.' She reaches for the king's hand, her cold fingers brushing his. 'Never again will we be lonely. Not beside one another.'

Kitt looks down at where their hands meet.

'Mara . . .' She likes the sound of her name until a humorous chuckle follows. 'Your company has been very much appreciated, and I think we both learned something from one another. But . . .'

'But what?'

Death's voice grows chilled. She has heard a version of this speech before, from lips that look like his.

'But,' he sighs out, 'you are Death.'

Mara's foot ceases its tapping.

'I didn't want to meet you.' Kitt says this in the way humans shrug – casually and without thought. 'I mean, you can't fault me for that. And I've enjoyed our time together, but we can't *be* together.' He offers an apologetic look. 'You do understand that, right?'

Oh, Death understands. All too well.

She yanks her hand from the king's with an icy fury. 'You think you are too good for me?'

'I didn't say that—'

Mara laughs, the sound sharp and so unlike her usual stoicism. The king startles at such an outburst. 'You think I am not precisely the power you seek?' Slowly, she stands to her feet. 'Few are lucky enough to behold me and live. But none are so foolish as to deny me.'

Kitt lifts his hands, as though Death is a creature to be tamed. 'Mara, I know you.' He holds her frigid gaze. 'I am not afraid—'

'You should be!' she snarls. Her frozen heart is breaking in two, and the feeling is painfully familiar. 'I am your Death, and it will not be kind.'

The king clutches his chest then, wincing at the pain that pulses there. 'Mara . . . please.'

'I will not be made a fool,' she seethes. 'Not again!' For the first time, Kitt can see every emotion crashing into her features. She wears it all — hurt, betrayal, the memory of a moment that mirrors this one. 'You may not want me, but Life no longer wants you.' Death leans over the desk, skewering Kitt to his seat. 'Your soul is *mine*. And what is left of me could have been yours,' she murmurs. 'But now, I won't be so gentle.'

Mara is not a monster — unless you make her out to be one.

As she vanishes from the study, Death is reminded of her abhorrence for the living. They are just as fickle as the fate that toys with them. Yes, whatever part of Mara longed — a rhythm to revive her heart, a loving caress to warm her cheek, a green gaze to look her way — has died all over again.

Her heart is a coffin.

And any man she lets inside will surely meet their doom.

Fondly, Mara thinks on this.

Not quite a monster, no.

But revenge is certainly a bitch.

CHAPTER 27

Kitt

I am drifting somewhere dark.

Healers crowd my study.

They pass a pitying look between themselves.

He's dying, their eyes say.

I know, respond my sunken ones.

Then, there is nothing.

Nothing.

Nothing.

I blink back into myself. Several new letters scatter the desk.

They spell out Calum's death at my hand.

I trace the morbid truth with my gaze, realizing I've turned a daughter into a fellow orphan.

I would tell Mara why, I had to, if she hadn't already vanished.

My gaze lifts from the page.

Death stands before me.

My mind is hazy. Her words swim in and out of my comprehension.

She wants to be with me.

I must have heard her wrong.

She is Death. I tell her so.

Mara does not take that well.

I was beginning to think her reputation was unwarranted.

But Death is deserving of the fear she so easily earns.

My head aches. My chest constricts.

I did precisely what I wished to prevent – make an enemy of Death.

Nothingness follows.

Then, my brother.

He stands beside my wife. The sight is unsurprising.

'She killed your father, not mine,' I hear Kai say, his voice muffled in my ears.

The Plague loosens its grip long enough for me to hear his damning words.

'Paedyn is more your family than I am.'

I'm drifting again, overwhelmed by the traitorous power consuming me.

No. No, no, no – I need to speak to my brother.

I rage against the darkness.

Please!

I'm sinking into oblivion.

Let me out! Let me out!

I need my brother. I need to know what I'm saying to him—

Nothing.

When I wrestle myself free from the Plague's clutches, there is a sword in my hand.

I lift the blade to block the stoker Kai brandishes.

He is panting. So am I.

We are sparring.

We are smiling.

We are falling back into a familiar, lethal dance.

I fight to remain in this moment with him.

But it fades like all the others.

It's a sudden burst of pain that pulls me back into the present.

I lift my bleary gaze.

Kai stands at the end of the stoker he holds.

But it is Death who drives it into my chest.

She wears a twisted grin, her cold hands wrapped around the iron shaft.

Mara, with the gentle smile. Mara, with the flour on her nose. Mara, with the heartbeat I lent her.

Mara, vengeance incarnate, guides that stoker through my flesh.

She is my Death.

'No!' Kai cries. 'You were supposed to dodge, Kitt!'

I prod at the wound, staining my fingers with blood.

'I . . . forgot.'

Just as I've forgotten everything.

My brother catches me when I fall.

This is not how I imagined it – dying.

The Plague curls up in the corner of my mind, letting me enjoy these last few moments of life.

I don't feel the pain. Not really.

This is relief.

Death stands over Kai's shaking shoulders, her pretty face unfeeling.

I cling to my fading soul.

I am with my brother. I don't want to be anywhere else.

'I wrote you l-letters,' I eventually say. Mara's presence grows stronger in my tightening chest. 'So you can see why I'm . . . a monster.'

I need him to know. Love me still. Forever. Always.

For him, I would do it all over again.

'It is time,' Death says coldly.

I lift my blurring gaze to her.

'I'll go gently. For you.'

There is no flash of light.

No bang or slow fade.

Kitt (now only a soul) feels cheated.

A presumably long while after Kitt's foretold demise (he no longer has any concept of time, you see), Death disturbs his peace.

He was just getting used to it, actually – the nothingness of it all. Only two stars keep him company, though often at a comfortable distance. Yes, the late king is alone, but decidedly not lonely. Not like he was among the living.

Kitt is sitting within the nuzzling nothingness – neither up, nor down, nor anything at all – when Mara steps into the darkness beside him. She wears a look that one would assume, justifiably, accompanies Death – bleak and cold. The pretty features the king once passively admired are now vacant of any emotion, deader than perhaps even she.

Her hollow gaze flicks over him with a chilling indifference. 'Are you enjoying your peace?'

Kitt nods, weary of this volatile Death. 'I am beginning to. It's quiet.' He quite likes that, he realizes. 'My mind hasn't been quiet in a while.'

'Good.' The word is cutting from Mara's tongue. She doesn't sound happy for him; rather, morbidly excited at the vulnerability of his enjoyment. And when a smile touches her cold lips, Kitt fears for the life he no longer has. 'Now I get to rip such peace away from you.'

The fallen king blinks at his grinning demise. 'What?'

'I only showed you such peace so I could take it away,' Death informs coolly. She then tilts her head at him, a habit that Kitt once found curiously endearing. 'Did you really think I would allow you the quietness you so crave?'

Kitt stands to his feet in the void. 'I . . . I don't understand.'

(There is much he has yet to comprehend. Most of all, the significance of Mara's seemingly sudden hatred for him, or rather, the Azer it belonged to long before. Loathing often finds a way to recognize itself in another. And in this lifetime, it has latched onto a different pair of green eyes, though they say the same thing when meeting Death's – she cannot possibly be loved.)

'I warned you Death would not be kind – *I* would not be kind,' Mara snarls, and the darkness quivers around her. She draws a breath then, one Kitt suspects she does not need. Then, leisurely, that worrisome smile returns to her lips. 'And now, you possess more of me than any other soul.'

Kitt knows he is not meant to understand this, and that frightens him greatly. 'Mara, please . . .'

'You were always meant to be king, Kitt.' Grinning, Death grabs his arm. 'Just not of Ilya.'

CHAPTER 28

Mara

5 Years Later

Mud hugs the hem of Mara's cloak.

With that green-eyed distraction now a degraded soul at her disposal, Death happily returns to her eternity. She spends every waking hour (which are all of them as a creature who never sleeps) collecting souls with a newfound apprentice and accompanied detachment. Mara has learned from her mistakes – in this lifetime, at least.

The passing of an elderly man leads Death to Tando. She walks along the spiritual plane until finding his still body tucked away in a quaint cottage. His wife is still weeping over the rather peaceful-looking corpse when Mara tugs his soul free from it. He protests as Death leads him from the home – only because he wishes to say goodbye

to the wailing woman. Mara might have found this sweet if she still believed in love.

So she herds the soul down quiet streets and between neat, brick buildings. That is, until a distantly familiar voice has Death stalling.

'. . . you're useless, gingersnap.'

'I honestly don't know what you expected, sending me to get your ingredients.'

'Yes, silly of me to think you would actually get anything on my list.'

Mara rounds the corner, ignoring the grumbling soul behind.

There, striding towards her, is the Tele and her Imperial.

Blair's lilac hair is swallowed by the hood of her cloak, but the scars climbing up one side of her face are worn proudly. Lenny walks beside her, nearly unrecognizable without that starchy uniform. His hair is longer, clothes plain, an arm slung around his former assignment's shoulders.

'Get off me,' she orders, attempting to shove him away. But the Hyper clings to her closely, even daring to plant a kiss to her temple.

Blair hides her smile with a sound of disgust, but there is no denying it – their souls are irrevocably intertwined. Yes, a vibrant glow of green and gold swirls around them, tangling into one.

Death stares at them in disbelief (and she might have even shown it on her face).

Because, after all this time, they are still doomed.

Lenny, grinning widely, has nearly passed Mara when his eyes suddenly meet hers.

Death stills.

He smiles.

'Good morning.'

To some, this is a simple, polite greeting. To Mara, this is the first acknowledgment she has received in years. And all because a Hyper found his sixth sense.

Blair glances vaguely in Death's direction before scoffing at gingersnap (which is most assuredly an endearing name now). 'Who the hell are you talking to?'

'The nice lady,' Lenny murmurs. 'Don't be rude just because you didn't get your sifted flour or whatever.'

Mara simply blinks at the apologetic look he throws over his shoulder.

She listens to them bicker (some things never change, it seems) as they stroll down the street and stop before a corner shop. It is a bakery, Death realizes.

Blair dons an apron beyond the large window. Lenny ties it for her.

It is *their* bakery.

Mara, rather begrudgingly, feels . . . *something* at the sight of them. She doesn't really want to think on it, actually, because she fears what will be discovered. Perhaps happiness. Or worse — envying such a thing.

So, she carries on down the street with a soul destined for the Mors.

Mara expects no more interruptions, but the sudden tugging in her chest cannot be ignored. She follows it, fervently and without thought, because Death knows nothing but this something that calls to her.

A muted market street spans before her, but Mara's gaze cuts through the crowd.

There, with an ear of corn in hand, skips a little girl.

Her parents are a piece of Ilya.

One with silver hair, and the other with that intriguing soul.

But it is the child Death is drawn to.

She crouches before the girl, her hair glinting gray in the speckled sunlight.

'Hello, little one,' Mara says.

Her smile is bright in the face of Death. 'You have pretty hair,' the child says sweetly.

Paedyn takes her daughter's hand. 'Who are you talking to, Kit?'

This name has a smile curling the edges of Death's lips.

It is a bit uninspired, if you ask her.

Mara tilts her head at the girl and watches as the happy family strides past.

The girl and her promising soul wave goodbye to Death.

But this is not the last time they will meet.

Mara taps a steady rhythm with her boot. Though, she no

longer pretends the beat belongs to her heart. No, she now finds comfort in the lack of such fragility.

For she cannot be confined. Not by Life and certainly not by man.

But perhaps by a woman.

Death smiles.

She has finally met her match.

EPILOGUE

Kitt

The trees murmur as he passes beneath them, their mossy branches caressing his cloaked shoulders.

Kitt does not hear his mother's voice among them, for he knows not what to listen for. Her voice is a memory, so distant and delicate, that he would much prefer it stays within the confines of his mind. There, it is safe from the Mors.

The ground softens beneath his boots, giving way to mud as the spindly trunks begin to thin. Kitt passes, flippantly, a fellow king who tears madly at the chalky bark of a tree. It once riled him, the thought of an eternity of disregard from the father who despised him. But he has learned to enjoy the solitude of his role in the Mors — for he weaves unnoticed among the wailing souls. Now he finds his own peace in admiring the

deranged man that was once his everything.

For Kitt has watched – since the beginning of this eternity – his father futilely attempt to free Iris Moyra from her peace. Even now, blood trickles from the cracked fingernails of a once fearsome Edric Azer as he claws at the trunk of an unassuming tree. He seems rather confident that his wife lies within this one, Kitt observes.

(Though, in the end, they will never know. Kitt cannot tell his mother or little sister from any other peaceful soul embedded into the fabric of the Mors – for his power is limited. But, selfishly, he is grateful to not know where his loved ones rest. You see, Kitt Azer is embarrassed. He does not wish for them to see what has become of him.)

The ever-gray sky hangs low above Kitt's blond head, dull without a gilded crown adorning it. A sharp tug in his chest has his pace quickening – his afterlife is quite demanding. In fact, he has spent most of his eternity (so far) contemplating how it might have turned out differently. Perhaps, then, if he had offered Mara the companionship she so craved, he would not be a slave to the Mors now. Or perhaps this was Death's plan all along – only, she wished to have him and his affections. But Kitt has no love left to give.

(Did she not understand that he was nearly incapable of the feeling?)

Even still, she punishes him for such unrequited sentiment. And despite all Kitt now knows of the Plague and its truth, he remains at a loss for how it all came to be. Or rather, how it all began with Mara.

'Go watch her,' Death says upon Kitt's arrival to their usual meeting place. It is a particularly precarious patch of cracked earth they now stand opposite on. Mara keeps her distance, cold and indifferent. Kitt keeps his composure, foolishly hopeful for a friendship in the next lifetime, if he is lucky (and it is quite clear that he is not).

'Any specific reason?' he asks, knowing Mara may not deign to answer.

Surprisingly, she does. 'It's her birthday. I want to know what she is up to.'

Kitt does not question her further. Instead, he simply nods and shuts his eyes in concentration.

'Remember what I taught you,' Death adds despite herself. Because, buried somewhere deep within that frigid heart of hers, she still cares for the Azer. 'Lose control to it.'

Focusing on that kernel of shifting power within him, Kitt does as Death instructs. Yes, he awakens the drowsy formidability curled up between his ribs. And now he does not fight it. He understands it.

He melts from one plane to the next before his feet sink into plush carpet. It has gotten easier, the sickening sensation and the rushing of power. Though, he is but a fraction of Death herself — such an endeavor as this thoroughly drains him. But Kitt, who hates admitting such a thing, does not mind doing

Mara's bidding. It makes him feel something he rarely did when living – needed.

Panting, Kitt looks around, taking in what once was his home. The castle looks different, warmer than it had the last time Death ordered him to Ilya. He wonders, distantly, just how much time has passed since he drew his last breath in the study down the hall.

He sets a quick pace towards the girl's room, fearing whomever it is that has piqued Death's interest. He knows very little of this mysterious being – only vague details from the clipped conversations Mara allows. But Kitt was wrong to be fearless in the face of Death the first time, for it is fear that would have kept him alive.

The hallway curls around a corner, and Kitt follows before he finds himself faltering to a stop.

There, clutching a carton of plump blueberries, stands the only person Kitt Azer ever truly learned to love.

'. . . Kitty?'

Kai's gaze widens on the ghost of his brother, welling with tears. He trembles slightly, in a way the Enforcer rarely did when Kitt was alive. But he is a king now, and perhaps, strangely, that gives him the power to feel more freely.

'Is that really you?' Kai chokes, nearly laughing.

Kitt notices, distantly, that time has taken its toll on only one of them. Stubble now shadows Kai's strong jaw beneath the eyes creased with years of laughter. And not for the first time, Kitt feels cheated. It was he who was meant to grow old alongside his brother.

'You . . .' The servant of the Mors struggles to swallow the emotion clogging his throat. 'You can see me?'

Tears fall swiftly from Kai's gray eyes. 'Of course I can see you, Kitt – but I'm not sure why because I . . .'

In this moment, Kitt cares not for his death or life or what might have been. No, all that matters is what Kai thinks of him – in this life and the next. But even after all these years, Kai still sees his brother, not the monster he has become.

'It wasn't your fault,' the dead brother reassures.

'I could have saved you. You were sick but—'

'I was already dying, Brother,' Kitt murmurs, his voice breaking. 'Death was the one who drove that poker into my chest, not you.'

Kai runs a hand through his hair, displaying the strands beginning to gray at his temples. 'Death? I don't understand.' He almost laughs. 'Am I going mad?'

'No, Brother.' Kitt remembers how to smile for him. 'But I do wonder how you can see me.'

'I see you everywhere, Kitt. In every smile, every ripple of water, every blade that I can't bear to raise.' Kai steps forward, slowly. 'And now you're actually here—'

'I'm not here.' Tears stream down Kitt's cheeks when he squeezes those green eyes shut (the ones that got him into this mess in the first place). 'Not really.'

'Are you – shit, this is ridiculous – some kind of ghost?'

The dead king looks up at the living one before him. 'I am much worse.'

Kai reaches for a brother that evades his touch. 'Let me help you, Kitt. Please—'

'There is no help for me in the Mors.' The words are dull. 'I am Death – not in its entirety, but enough to make me useful. And it is all my doing.' Kitt shakes his head. 'I gambled with power, and it took control.'

The king stares unblinkingly at this Kitt before him, oddly familiar yet entirely unknown. 'The Plague,' he murmurs. 'Is that what did this to you?'

The sliver of Death does not answer. He too has become rather cryptic – an occupational hazard, it seems.

The king's voice grows stern. 'What is the Plague, Kitt?'

'You do not wish to know.'

Kai rubs at his tired eyes. 'I don't understand.'

'You are not meant to.'

'And you are Death?' The words are drenched in disbelief before a rush of realization swiftly washes them away. 'Am I going to die, Kitt? Is that why I can see you?'

The brothers behold each other for a moment that has even eternity shying away. For this bond is infinite.

'Not yet, Brother.'

And then Kitt is gone, tugged from that physical plane by his master.

He stumbles back into the Mors, where Mara awaits. She does not look at him.

'How is my prodigy?'

Kitt hardly hears the lie he spews. For his mind is far away, in the land of the living, where his heart ceased beating years ago.

Death seems pleased by his answer nonetheless. 'Good. We have much work to do.'

Her lips curl into that cruel smile. Then they form the mocking title she has bestowed upon him.

'Welcome home, King of the Mors.'

> Hunted. Hunter.
> Destined for each other.

Powerless

INTERNATIONAL BESTSELLING AUTHOR
LAUREN ROBERTS

**The first in the instant
New York Times bestselling series**

Be swept away by the second heart-racing instalment in this bestselling and sizzling fantasy romance trilogy

*Betrothed. Betrayed.
Destined for each other?*

Fearless

NO.1 INTERNATIONAL BESTSELLING AUTHOR OF *POWERLESS*
LAUREN ROBERTS

**The epic conclusion
to the sizzling fantasy romance series.**

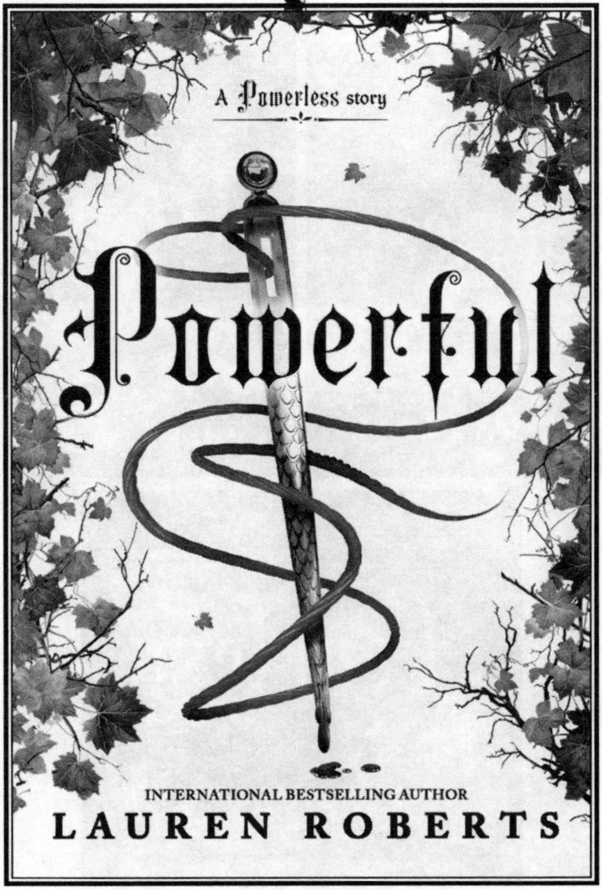

**An unmissable companion to
The *Powerless* series.**

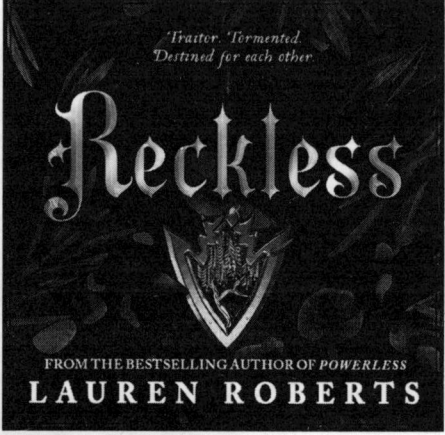
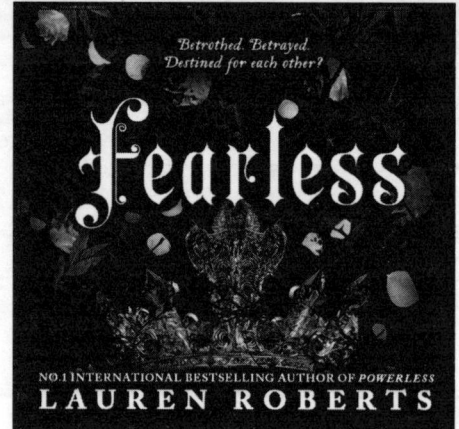

Available now in audiobook!

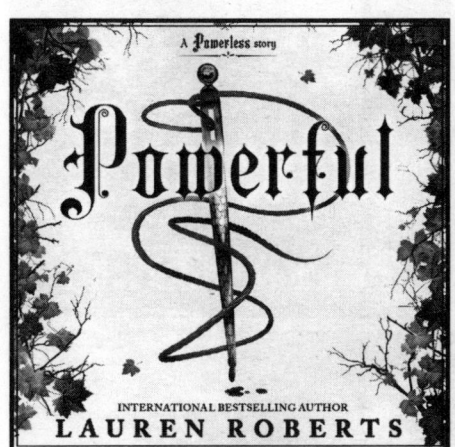
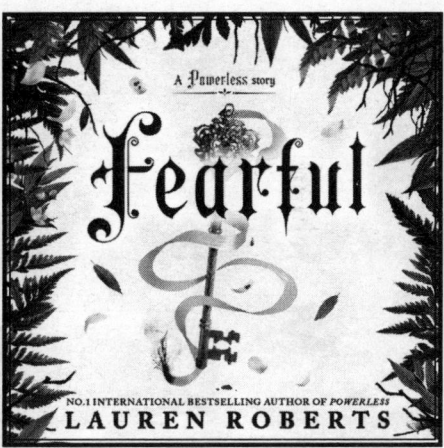

Also available now in audiobook!

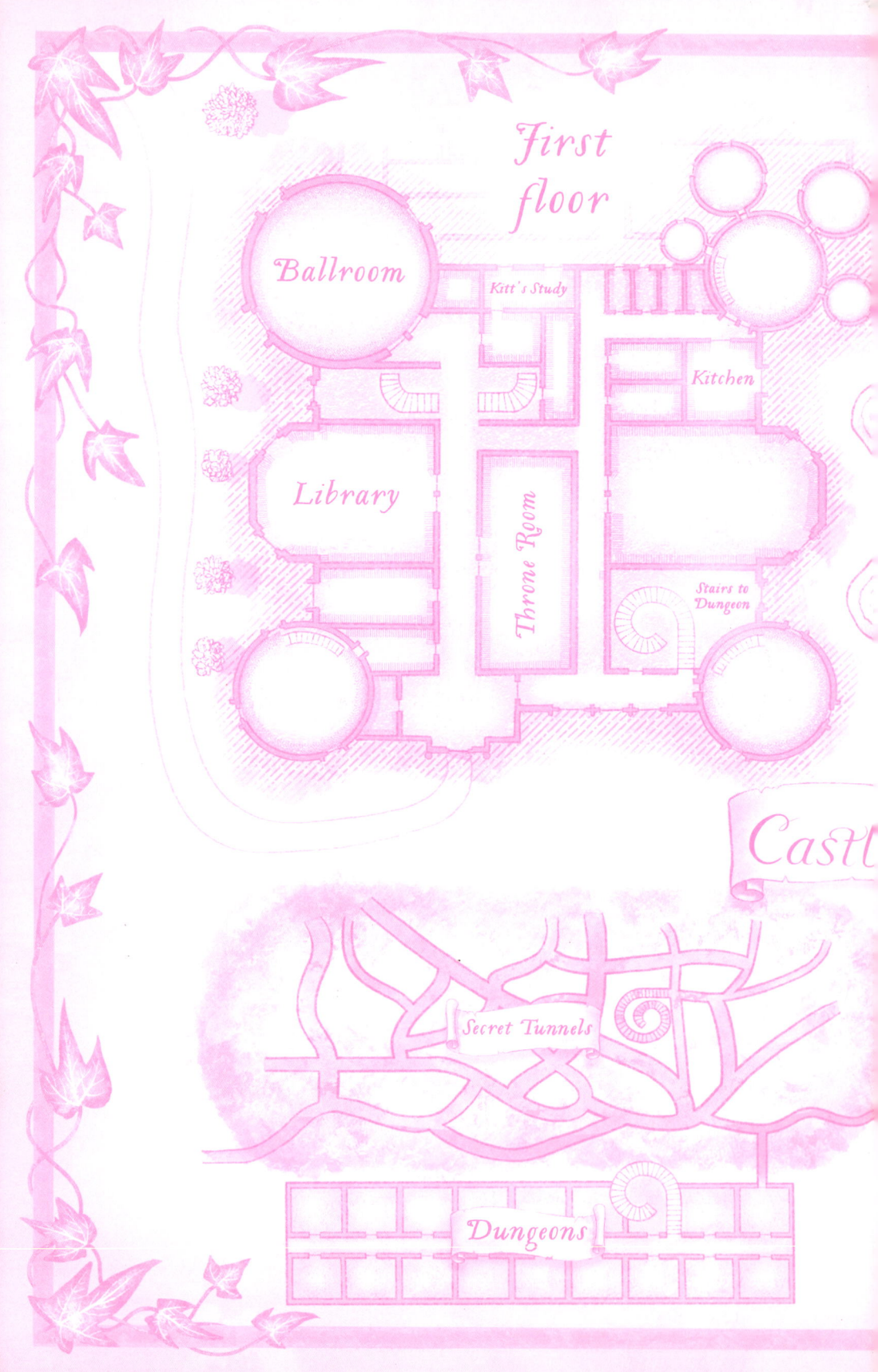